Hope

an ARIA Anthology

Selected short fiction, non-fiction, poetry & prose
from the Association of Rhode Island Authors

Hope: Selected short fiction, non-fiction, poetry & prose from the Association of Rhode Island Authors

Produced and printed
by Stillwater River Publications.

Visit our website at
www.StillwaterPress.com
for more information.
First Stillwater River Publications Edition

ISBN: 978-1-952521-27-0

Library of Congress
Control Number: 2020941637

1 2 3 4 5 6 7 8 9 10
A publication of the Association
of Rhode Island Authors(ARIA)
Cover design by Emma St. Jean.
Published by Stillwater River Publications,
Pawtucket, RI, USA.

The views and opinions expressed in this book are solely those of the author and do not necessarily reflect the views and opinions of the publisher.

Table of Contents

Hope

Introduction

This is the fifth annual anthology of works from the Association of Rhode Island Authors, a three-hundred-plus member group of poets and writers. For 2020, I chose a theme, which is also our state's motto: HOPE. When I selected 'Hope' as our theme last fall, I had no idea how timely it would be. With a global pandemic at the beginning of the year, followed by social unrest and calls for change, and with many of us feeling anxious, uncertain, frustrated, and even desperate, 'hope' is a chance to find light in these dark days. For some writers, finding hope was indeed a challenge, and hope can, of course, be interpreted in many different ways.

But there is hope in these works, even though it may not always be outwardly apparent. Whether that hope is manifested in optimism, faith, concern, or simple wishes, we believe you will find this selection of prose and poetry uplifting, soothing, and comforting.

Our Association of Rhode Island Authors is a talented group! There's a diversity of writers and poets here, and it was truly a joy to see what they came up with this year. Some of our writers and poets submit something every year, and for others, it was a first-time venture. Perhaps this is the first time you have something published – if so, congratulations! You are a published author! That's an accomplishment worth sharing with everyone you know. And if your submitted piece was not chosen this year, please try again next year.

It was an honor to serve as chair and editor for this year's anthology. Our dedicated panel of volunteer judges took on the difficult task of reading and reviewing dozens of submissions, and determining the works that ultimately would be included in this anthology.

I *hope* you enjoy this year's compendium – and it is my *hope* that you find solace, satisfaction, and contentment as you read. Honoré de Balzac said, "Reading brings us unknown friends." Through this anthology, you may discover an unknown author, and isn't that a gift?
Be well.

Martha Reynolds,
Chair and Editor, ARIA Anthology

Moments in Between

by Jill Fague

The house feels much too still for a weeknight in March. Nobody bustles in or out. Nobody interacts. Quiet stretches the monotonous night. Surrendered to our preferred spots, everyone seems to be biding time, like waiting at the back of a line that never moves. No matter how patient, we simply cannot make our way to the front. Even if we did, would anything be left in the wizard's bag for a high school senior? There's no place to go. No one to see. Nothing to do. Just another empty evening in the duration of many, but somehow tonight sharpens the edges of our collective disappointment.

Tonight should have been my daughter Riley's senior festival concert, one of her last high school performances and one of the final times she would ever play her flute. She is not a gifted musician. She does not even like playing the flute all that much. So why is it crushing me that her concert was cancelled? That shiny flute. The sight of it gets me. Every time.

When Riley started fifth grade, word came home that our local elementary school was implementing a new band program. My husband and I encouraged Riley to try an instrument. The band meeting rolled around, the "mandatory" one in the evening where many parents just wanted to go home after a long day's work. The meeting that an email probably could have covered. Typically, that might have been my inner monologue, but instead I was content to sit in the cafeteria, to pretend life was normal for a moment. Having recently been diagnosed with cancer, I did not mind the distraction.

As the music store employee reviewed the instruments and the available purchase contracts, I experienced sticker shock. I hoped Riley would not pick an instrument with a price tag resembling our monthly mortgage. I was not prepared to disappoint her, but I also felt unprepared to make a big investment. Listening to the presentation, my mind drifted. I worried about my medical bills. *How much were my upcoming treatments going to cost? Was my family headed for financial disaster?* Suddenly, the cafeteria felt stuffy and way too small. So much for a distraction or sense of normalcy.

What if Riley simply hated playing the instrument she chose, or she couldn't play it well? That was entirely possible. We are not the most musical family. I mean, we love music as much as the next people, but I do believe my half of Riley's DNA includes a gene for tone deafness. And do not even get me started on my rhythm. Embarrassing. Based on my husband's guitar lessons, he is not exactly a gifted musician either. It's safe to say our household does not miss his practice sessions.

Riley decided to try the flute. It had a nice enough sound. I mean, anything was better than that wretched third-grade recorder. And it was small enough for our little peanut to carry. Sounded like a plan. A short time later, I purchased my friend's daughter's flute. Her daughter was all grown up and her family was purging their home, so the flute lost its spot on their sentimental shelf. One hundred dollars later, we owned an intermediate flute, case and all. A win-win. Riley could try the instrument, and if she didn't like it, no harm done. Since the flute had a nice new home, my friend's daughter didn't feel too guilty about parting with it either.

After school one day, I watched Riley riding her bike in the driveway. Suddenly, recalling the grave injustice served to her, she stomped her foot down and declared, "The clarinets learned the E note today, and all we did was learn how to blow!" Indignant, she recounted the criminal behavior of her fellow woodwinds. Consequently, the innocent flute players lost their chance to learn a new note. Rooked by her delinquent fifth grade classmates, those little ratscallions. Thoroughly amused by her word choice, I figured we were doing okay if that was her only complaint of the day. Of course, Riley remained totally unaware of my silent, malignant enemy at the time.

Fast forward, one year later. I walked into the crowded, stuffy, middle school gym for Riley's school concert. Spying my tiny daughter perched on her folding chair, clad in the obligatory black and white band outfit, flute in hand, I suddenly felt this incredible sense of peace and gratitude. I had been swept up in a tornado of cancer treatments over the previous year and landed in this exact spot. There was no place like the middle school gym.

From the bleachers, I sent up a silent prayer of thanks and hoped to see this precious little girl graduate from high school one day. I did not want to miss another moment or to imagine any of Riley's future moments stolen by my untimely demise. Seeing my daughter with that flute somehow grounded my thoughts. I felt changed: no longer the impatient parent wishing to be elsewhere, thinking about the next task, watching the clock and resenting the rest of the night's demands. Nothing else mattered in that moment. Just my girl and her flute.

Every concert since has been a milestone. Another day, another month, another year I have had the pleasure of being Riley's mom. Recently, she and her friends have taken to calling me "Momma J," which I secretly love. The transition from "Mommy" to "Mom" made me sad as my children grew into teenagers, so my new nickname rekindled a tiny bit of joy in my heart.

Many parents of older girls warned me about the teenage years. How my sweet child would morph into a cranky, unrecognizable she-beast. Not my Riley. I can count on one hand the number of times we have truly fought, and I would have fingers left over. When my mother and I fought, she frequently shouted, "I hope you have a kid just like you!" I'm not sure if that was an Irish curse or what, but she took great satisfaction wishing it upon me. In the best possible way, Riley is not like me, at least not like my teenage self. She is even-tempered, kind, and she does not need to have the last word. Imagine that.

Throughout Riley's high school years, it did not matter how tired I felt, how busy I was, or how much I froze waiting for that band float in the annual December holiday parade. Those nights always gave me a reason to remember how fortunate I was to share my daughter's life. That simple flute marked the passage of time, a testimonial to Riley's growth and confidence, a steady symbol of hope. It reminded me how blessed I was to see my daughter grow up, each step closer to her high school graduation and more.

We never bought a replacement flute. A few times it needed an adjustment by a professional, but it held up. And since Riley wasn't serious about playing it, we never considered an upgrade. It's safe to say that flute doesn't owe us anything after eight faithful years. Eight years of treasured moments with my girl.

Now here we are. Riley's senior year. Suddenly, my daughter's moments have been stolen, but not for the reason I feared. *A world-wide pandemic? Didn't see that one coming.* Witnessing Riley's grief over her senior year sends me straight back to the hopelessness I felt when she started fifth grade. Anger and uncertainly have replaced her joy, and she has lost her balance, but this time she is not riding her pink bike in the driveway. It will take more than a Band-Aid on a skinned knee to right her world.

Everything she has worked for seems lost. Having been accepted to all ten colleges where she applied, Riley's senior stress was finally paying off. All the fun was just beginning. She was looking forward to Honors Night, festival concert, prom, decision day, graduation, and her eighteenth birthday. But the universe had different plans. With the flick of its wand, all hopes for her senior year have vanished. Thank you, coronavirus.

I get it, my family is safe, but that does not make everyday life any easier as the parent of a high school senior. Each time I see Riley at her computer, engaged in her "remote learning," I am at once saddened by this unlikely turn of events and amazed by her resilience. In her slippers, I would not have completed a single virtual lesson. Since colleges have already sent acceptances, it is unlikely that any institution would rescind their offer at this point. *Hello, pandemic. What a perfect excuse for senioritis.*

I still might not see her graduate, not the way I envisioned, but maybe the end game is not what matters most. Maybe the moments in between the celebrations and the disappointments are the ones that really count. Our everyday moments. No misfortune can ever replace them. Like the moment one buys a flute.

Earlier this week, when my husband came home from work, he looked surprised to hear Riley practicing her flute. As he removed his tie, he tipped his head and asked, "She's playing her flute? Is that

Somewhere Over the Rainbow?" Pretty ironic. At the end of her ruined senior year, Riley was upstairs in her room recording a classic, optimistic song. *But what happened to her hopes? Her childhood lullabies?* I thought about my favorite childhood portrait of Riley and her little brother on the living room wall, the poster-sized one where they dressed as Dorothy and the Cowardly Lion for Halloween. Now here we are. Friends are not shaking hands, and the world is not wonderful. But Riley is still playing her hopeful tune.

She always hated band assessments and performing solo for the teacher. But she was still trying. *Why didn't she just give up? Who the heck cared right now?* Just refuse to do it, girl. That would have been my play at her age. *So, no Mom, my kid is not like me. She does not rebel. She does not lose her temper and disregard others. She does not sidestep her responsibilities.* When her hopes get derailed, Riley manages her emotions, stays focused, and charges forward. So maybe, just maybe, the Irish curse worked, and she is a little bit like me after all. Perhaps I have taught my daughter something about dealing with life's disappointments.

A few days ago, I watched Riley meticulously craft a card, color it, and place it next to her materials at the kitchen table where she has been completing homework for years. I wish I had logged her hours at that worn out table. The scratches on the hardwood under her chair attest to her dedication and time spent there.

I wondered why she cared about that card so much. It said, "hello" on the cover in beautiful, black script that almost looked computer generated. It was just so perfect. *Did she honestly give a care about her art grade right now? Why did my kid have to waste her time on this? What was the point?* I resented the time she spent making it. Here we were in the middle of a world-wide pandemic. Her father was a first responder. Riley had better things to worry about. She was also in the middle of scholarship applications, a tedious, time-consuming process. The poor kid had eye strain from all the screen time. *Did she really need art busywork on top of everything else?* Watching her painstaking efforts, as she added some finishing touches to her card this evening, I felt my annoyance growing.

"Sweetpea, who is that card for?" I finally asked.

"Someone in a nursing home," came her matter-of-fact reply.

Well, there you have it.

Tonight, we are not at a concert. Riley is neither on stage with her flute nor celebrating her senior year. But I could not feel any prouder of my daughter in this moment. In this moment, when she has every right to feel angry or bitter, she is bringing a smile to someone else's face. And hopefully that smile will be the only contagious thing in that nursing home.

Dark Bittersweet

By Richard Maule

Every part of me felt like staying home, but it was Sunday and the people at LifePrime Convalescent Center would be expecting somebody. Mama was the one who usually visited Miriam Longmire, but Mama died on Tuesday, leaving me with a heavy heart and a long list of things to be done. I knew Mama would want me to put Miriam at the top of her list. It fell on me to tell Miriam her best friend was dead. On the drive over, I racked my brain for some pleasant way to break the bad news.

Miriam and Mama had known each other since they were girls. They both had a zillion old stories – of paper dolls, school dances, and heartbreaking details of the Great Depression. Each had been maid of honor at the other's wedding. (I should say wedding*s*, since they had both had two.) Both first husbands had died in World War II. Miriam's second, Jake Longmire, was a business partner of Dad, my mother's second. The two men were never close like Mama and Miriam, but they both managed to pass away in the same week ten years ago, both of heart attacks. Mama's stories rarely touched on anything that happened after that.

The years that followed were difficult for both women. Being a buoyant soul, Mrs. Longmire managed to keep her childlike cheerfulness, even through multiple cancers and joint replacements. Her teeth were a mess too, but that didn't stop her from flashing her huge smile, stains, crowns, and all.

Mama's teeth fared better, but smiling was never her thing. In her widowhood, Mama took up complaining the way some old ladies take up knitting. She pointed out every flaw in the world until the world, and pretty much all her friends, learned to keep their distance. Everyone, that is, except Miriam Longmire. I knew Miriam wouldn't care if I showed up on visiting day in Mama's stead. Miriam got along with everybody.

I was surprised to find so many free spaces in visitor parking. A couple of families were coming out of the building, all of them smiling and talking. They seemed relieved to have fulfilled their duty to whichever patient they had come to see. LifePrime referred to the patients as *residents*, of course, but Mama always called them *inmates*. She was outraged that anyone should have to weather their final years in such a place.

I took my time trudging up the sidewalk that wound through the flower beds. In truth, there weren't any real flowers, just a few plastic ones lined up like tombstones amidst the weeds. As I approached the front door, I noticed a stack of fresh mail and glamour magazines by the employees' entrance. There was no mail by the lobby door though, just some boxes of paper towels and incontinence supplies.

I was glad I remembered to bring the gift bag Mama had bought for Miriam, but even Sterling chocolates would be inadequate to soothe the wound I was about to deliver. "Let's do this," I whispered to myself. Then I took a deep breath and stepped inside.

The lobby stank of floral air freshener, but no institutional perfume could mask the smell of soiled bedsheets and bleach. A line of wheelchairs had been parked in front of the back window that faced the shopping mall, but every occupant was sleeping.

While I waited to sign in, a middle-aged woman in front of me whispered, "God, the place stinks of death."

Not wanting to seem rude, I faked a smile and lowered my eyes. As I stared down into my shiny bag of chocolate, I couldn't stop thinking about what the lady had said. I was still trying to come up with a fitting reply when my turn came. I told the receptionist I was there to visit Miriam Longmire in 318, but the woman didn't even turn from the talk show she was watching.

I went ahead and signed in, careful to specify my full name and purpose. Still hearing no response, I repeated what I had said before, louder this time.

"No need to shout, sweetie," snapped the woman. "I'm not a resident. You want 318. Third floor, left, halfway down the hall."

I knew better than to say anything. The receptionist's name was on her shirt, but I knew this Louise from my previous visits. Like most of the LifePrime staff, she never remembered anybody. I guess in a place like this, it's better if you don't let yourself get too attached. I was going to say thank you, but Louise had already turned back to her show. I just rolled my eyes and marched off toward the elevator.

The "stinks of death" woman was already there, but thankfully said nothing this time. We waited together in silence for a full three minutes, both pretending we were checking out text messages. When the door finally swooshed open, the elevator was empty. "Remind me not to depend on this one in a fire," I joked.

But the woman didn't smile. "Three," was all she said.

I nodded and pushed the button for both of us.

At the third floor, we got off and went in opposite directions, each of us eager to complete our respective missions. The hall was clean and quiet, and it had a different bad smell from the lobby. The only decorations on the walls were the fire instructions and a single glamorized picture of the building's front entrance.

When I got to 318, I looked down at my phone to doublecheck the number, but I knew I was in the right place. "Knock, knock!" I said as I fondled the rope handles of my gift bag. There was no reply, so I rapped politely on the half-opened door and eased myself in.

Miriam was in her bed, flat on her back but wide awake. Her face was more haggard than I remembered, but her blue-white hair looked like it had just been permed. "Hello, Miriam," I said cheerily. "It's Kate Greenwood… Evelyn's daughter."

"I know who you are, dear," she replied. "Your mother shows me your picture every Sunday."

"You must have a sharp eye for faces," I said. "Mama's snapshots are all from twenty years ago when I lived at home."

Miriam grinned. "A mother always sees her little girl," she said. Without looking, she reached down for the switch that made her bed growl up to chair-angle. "There," she said as her blue eyes twinkled squarely into mine. "Back in the land of the living!"

"Welcome back." I smiled as I took her hand. It was cold and boney, but softer than I had expected. As Miriam tightened her fingers on mine, I said, "You've got quite a grip there… and I just love your hair."

"Thank you," she cooed. "The perm is still fresh enough to stink." As we both chuckled, Miriam added, "The students from Lawrence and Ryder come every Friday to practice on us old ladies."

"Lawrence and Ryder?"

"Part of Phipps," she said, "the undertaker college. The students are learning to spiff up corpses for funerals. They figure we already look the part."

Fearing it would seem impolite to laugh, I just gave a demure nod. "Well, Miriam, you look lovely in any case."

"I think *lifelike* is the look they're after," she laughed. "Gawd, Kate, you're an insufferable diplomat… a much nicer liar than your mother."

"Mama always did call a spade a spade," I said without thinking. I realized I had just referred to my mother in the past tense, but Miriam gave no hint that anything was amiss. She had no inkling that her best friend was gone.

"Your mama can be a witch with a capital B." She smiled. "But you always know where you stand."

I nodded, but for some reason, I blurted out the first thing that came into my head. "But a home should be a place of peace, don't you think?"

Miriam just frowned. "Gawd… sounds boring," she said.

"Mama is sorry she couldn't make it today," I said. It was a lie, but at least I was using the present tense now. "She said I should tell you… she loves you."

"Nonsense," said Miriam. "Your mama said no such thing. She hasn't said anything that mushy since your dad died. Old friends like us don't need *I love yous*."

Feeling cornered and nervous, I tried to pull my hand back, but Miriam's grip only tightened. "Relax, dear," she said. "I don't bite. And I can see your mother *next* Sunday."

"Next Sunday…" I repeated. As my heart began to skip beats, I could almost hear Mama's voice commanding me to announce her passing and be done with it. But as I stared into Miriam's eyes, my heart wouldn't let me drop the bomb. The old lady's smile was as giddy as Christmas. She may have been half-ditsy from age and medications, but how could I shatter her happiness with such tragic news? The truth be damned, I thought. Truth can wait.

Mercifully, Miriam finally let go of my hand. Unobserved, I silently used it to check my pulse. God, my heart was a drumroll. All morning I had been dreading having to tell Mrs. Longmire that Mama was dead. Now I was terrified because I had seemingly made the decision *not* to. I'm a chicken, I thought to myself.

"I'm so glad it worked out for me to come today," I said sweetly, but every part of me wanted to toss Miriam her candy and make a mad dash for the door. My eyes began to flash between every ordinary object in the room – the wall clock, the bedpan on the floor, and the clipboard Velcroed to the foot of the bed. But when I looked back at Miriam, she was calm and still smiling. She had swallowed the lie – hook, line, and sinker.

"Your visit is an unexpected blessing," she said.

"I doubt I'm much of a blessing," I said as I handed Miriam her chocolates, "but Mama says you like Sterling."

Miriam stuck her nose into the gift bag and inhaled. "Gawd, your Mama's an angel."

An *angel,* right. Miriam's words were truer than she knew. But with each passing moment, I was getting more comfortable pretending that Mama was still around. I went on to tell Miriam how well Mama was doing – her bridge club victories, her glowing medical checkup, and her recent outing to the botanical garden. All of it was made up, of course, but by now I was on a roll. My conscience occasionally tried to interrupt, but I kept telling myself a polite lie was a double blessing – soothing both to the liar and the one lied to. And God knows, Miriam was not going to know any better. My heartbeat was finally beating normally.

Her smile widened as I told old stories of Mama and me – the Girl Scout hikes, giggling at the movies, and us whispering secrets to each other at bedtime. I described how Mama had gushed over what a knock-out I was in my prom dress. The pictures I painted for Miriam were not reality, but God were they pretty. I was describing Mama and me as I had always dreamed we might be. Old Miriam sighed at every little detail, and soon, I was sighing too.

My stories had taken my mind back to places I hadn't visited in years. My neck stiffened as I recalled the horrible things my mother really had said about that prom dress. "Too flat-chested for that neckline, too wide in the hips." In my head, I could still hear every word, but I saw no reason to mention it to Miriam.

"Mama always pushed me to go out for sports and such," I said, "but I never tried. Sometimes I suspect I did it just to spite her."

At first, I wondered if Miriam had heard me, but then she frowned. "Spite's a pretty lame roadmap for a person's life," she said. "Your mother saw possibilities in you that you were afraid to explore. She was a go-getter, you know. She just never got the chance to go and get."

Afraid to reply, I just launched into more stories, true ones this time. Some of them were even pleasant. I told how Mama had marched into Principal Thielen's office and given him hell for not recommending me to UCONN. She and I sang the school fight song as together we keyed Thielen's black Chevrolet. It seemed so silly now, but what a day – me and Mama, partners in crime. Other good memories began to flood my brain. I described the night Mama got drunk with me after I got fired from my first job. And there was the afternoon she and I prayed together at Daddy's grave. God, how much I had forgotten. Miriam laughed, but I was choking up.

Realizing I was getting weepy, I decided to shut down this cavalcade of sentimentality and go back to lying. I spent ten minutes detailing a fake romance I was having with a guy named Carl Branning (a fiancée I had just invented). I told Miriam that Mama was wanting me and Carl to have a fancy honeymoon, but I didn't want to waste the money.

I expected Miriam to rebuke my stodginess, but when I looked over, she had nodded off. Not knowing how to work the bed, I just left her in the upright position, snoring like a sailor. She looked so peaceful I almost envied her.

The drive home was a blur. I felt silly to have wasted so much time spinning yarns and even sillier that I had enjoyed them so much. I had successfully warmed an old lady's heart with a blanket of lies, but now what? Mama would never visit LifePrime again. Was I going to put myself through this ordeal Sunday after Sunday?

I had chickened out of breaking the bad news, I now needed a plan. My first thought was to come back next week and just blurt out that Mama was dead. The old lady would probably not even remember today's visit. But then again, she might.

By bedtime, I had talked myself into keeping the ruse going. Miriam took so much delight in my stories; it would be cruel not to let her hang onto Mama a little bit longer. After all, how many more lucid days did she have left?

The wisdom of this approach seemed to be affirmed in the Sundays that followed. These visits with Miriam turned out to be to be a sublime joy, and in many ways, a revelation. I discovered I was an excellent storyteller with an excellent memory for detail. Every week, I would make up a new excuse about why Mama hadn't come, but Miriam never seemed to connect the dots. My company and my stories seemed to be enough for her.

And Miriam could spin a pretty good yarn herself. She talked about her life and her husbands, but my favorite stories were about her adventures with Mama. She described how they had installed seats on B-26 bombers during the war. "I barely got the hang of it," she said, "but your mother was Rosie the Riveter. She taught me to chug beer and play cards after work. Evelyn said with the boys gone, it fell on us to keep the bars in business." Miriam's tales were delightful, and she could hardly stop herself. In truth, I didn't want her to stop.

As it turned out, there was more to Mama than I had known. As a teen she had dreamed of becoming a lawyer. She was captain of her high school swim team that won the state championship her senior year. But then the war changed everything. Mama started drinking heavily after her first husband died, and when Daddy passed, she even contemplated suicide. She told Miriam I would have a better chance in life without a grumpy drunk for a mother.

I began to understand why my mother had spoken so little of her life, and especially of her secrets. Then I started to wonder if I was the kind of daughter a mother could confide in. There was so much of Mama I had not known, and so much I would never know. God, I wished I had taken the risk to ask her more.

Since Miriam was my only source of reliable information. I went on deceiving her for almost a year, laughing, listening, sometimes not even caring what was true or false. But the big lie was always there, looming like a distant storm cloud behind every conversation. I started to see questions lurking behind Miriam's blue eyes.

I said nothing about it, of course, but things changed the day Miriam up and asked, "Gawd, child. What are you running from?"

After a long silence, I tossed Miriam a few awkward words. "It's Mama," I whispered. "I always wonder if she is pleased with me… if I am falling short."

"She wonders the same about you," she said. Miriam then told me how often Mama bragged about my level-headedness, but that she had worried I would never find a man good enough for me. *Level-headed* seemed like a back-handed compliment, but I suspected my mother had been right. She had been right about a lot of things.

I wanted to fend Miriam off with more contrived stories, but instead, I decided to be honest about what I could be honest about. I told her how lonely I was, and that on my fortieth birthday, I had surrendered to the notion that I was never going to get in shape and that I wasn't cut out for relationships. I fully expected this confession to win me sympathy, but Miriam for once took off her sweet face. She got so mad she cranked the bed all the way up.

"Nonsense!" she barked. "You just have to take people as they are… men especially."

"I can't," I said. "With every friend and every man it starts the same. Good at first, then things gradually go south. Things get boring, then prickly, and in the end, explosive. Believe me, Miriam, I've tried."

"Oh, you *tried*, did you," she whined. "Listen, girlie… a person can't just *try* to fall head over heels. You want to *try* something, go try on shoes in a store. Even then you can't know anything until you've worn them a while. Kate, you're just a big fraidy cat."

"Just shut up and eat your chocolate." I smiled, but there was no way of escape. I turned toward the window so Miriam couldn't see my tears. An avalanche of thoughts was crushing in from every side. I probably should have thanked Miriam, but part of me wanted to scream. I wanted to tell her Mama was dead and all this storytelling was just a big sentimental charade. I could just press a pillow over her face and leave us all in peace.

But damn that Miriam, she kept smiling, oblivious to the storm that was swirling in my heart. I pinched my lips shut, so tight they began to throb. I was looking in her general direction but wasn't looking her in the eyes. But when she began to pat the bed beside her, I finally exhaled.

"Come over here, dear," she said. "I want you to taste something." With two shaky fingers, Miriam pulled a piece of chocolate from her gift bag. I shook my head no, but she would have nothing of it. "Oh, Gawd!" she laughed. "What kind of woman turns down chocolate?"

Cornered, I took the candy, but I took my time unwrapping it. The silver foil had the word *Sterling Chocolatiers* embossed on it. I sniffed the almost black chocolate, then nibbled off a little taste. Miriam's gray brows furrowed.

"No, no!" she said firmly. "It only works if you chomp the whole thing."

I knew better than to fight her, so I closed my eyes and complied.

I guess nobody is ever ready for the amazing explosion good chocolate makes in your mouth. I pursed my lips, wagging my face as if I were saying no. I have no doubt that Eve did the same thing when she took her first bite of the forbidden fruit. The first word that popped into my unedited mind was *damn*, but "Wicked good," was what I whispered.

"Sterling calls it their *dark bittersweet*," she said. "It's my favorite. Your mom's, too."

"To die for." I smiled. "Funny, whenever Mama used to bring home a box of Sterlings, I always used to leave her the dark ones. I assumed they were bitter."

"You were young," Miriam said. "Children are stupid that way. They think the sweeter the better. But old folks know. We know it takes a tad of bitter to make good chocolate. Like life and love, it takes a mix of bitter and sweet."

"More please," I whined as I held out my hand like a little girl.

That chocolate was hands down the best I ever tasted – almost as good as Miriam's wise words. I kept coming back for more, both of chocolate and wisdom. And every Sunday I would secretly replenish Miriam's bag with fresh chocolates while she was jacking up her bed. She kept remarking how Sterling really gave you a generous bagful, but I suspected she was on to my trick.

For another year of Sundays, we shared our old stories, all of them true now. But gradually our conversations shifted to newer developments. I was promoted to department supervisor at work, and on my fiftieth birthday, I ran my first half marathon. During my training, I met an incredible man to whom I managed to get engaged. I still couldn't bring myself to tell Mariam this real one was named Timothy Brooks, not Carl Branning. Unlike me, Tim is an overly adventurous dreamer, a bit of a flake, but quite a guy in any case.

Tim and I got married that next fall, but before we flew off for two weeks in Mallorca, I told him I wanted to stop by LifePrime. I brought Miriam her magic chocolates, of course, plus some of the prettiest flowers from the wedding. I intentionally kept my bride's dress on for her to see.

"I knew you'd look beautiful in white," she said, "but it's your gorgeous smile that makes the outfit."

"Thanks!" I said. "I doubt I would smile at all without you, Miriam. And you would have adored Mama's dress."

Then, as we smiled into each other's eyes, Miriam's expression seemed to gradually sadden. "I'm so very happy for you, Kate," she said, almost whispering. "And how I wish your mama could have been here to see it."

It only took a few seconds for me to put two and two together. My eyes teared up and I gasped for air. Miriam knew about Mama. As my heart twisted in my chest, Miriam's blue eyes were also welling with tears. I saw love too, but I instinctively turned my face toward the window.

"God… all this time," was all I could think to say. "You knew she was gone and you still let me play the fool." My heart was wanting to run in every direction. Any direction. I felt trapped, angry, but mostly just busted. "How long did you know?" I finally asked.

As I waited for her reply, I pretended to stare at something in the mall parking lot. Miriam gave me a minute to stew in my juices.

"I saw the obituary right before your first visit," she answered. "I figured a stroke. When Evelyn stopped taking her meds, she and I both knew it was just a matter of time."

In that stark moment, I felt like I was drowning. I didn't want to turn and face Miriam, but I knew I couldn't walk away. Miriam had become my best friend in the world.

"Well, you certainly didn't let on," I said.

"I followed your lead, dear."

Though I was still looking out the window, I knew Miriam was smiling. "I'm sorry I deceived you," I whispered as I stared at the cars at the mall. "I suppose I was just trying to spare your feelings."

"It was all right, dear," she said. "I took it as love."

"But why did you let me keep on pretending?" I said as turned to face her. "Concocting all those stories! Sharing about everything Mama ever said and did."

"I savored every word, Kate." She smiled. "It cheered my heart. It kept Evelyn alive for me. I figured for you, too."

"I suppose it's good to finally end the charade," I said.

Miriam got quiet then. And for one of those rare moments, she wasn't smiling. When she finally did speak, her voice was serious and unfamiliar. "It wasn't silly at all," she sighed. "But it feels strange that it's all over – heavy. A bit like a death."

Mama really is gone now, I thought. Gone for both of us. "I shouldn't have tried to fool you," I said.

"You were trying to ease my pain."

"Ours," I said. "*Our* pain. I told myself the whole exercise was for you, but now I suspect it was more for me. I learned more about Mama in those stories than I did in a lifetime of busy years. Learned about myself as well. I suppose it's good to remember the wonderful things about the people we lose."

"I suppose," Miriam sighed. "But truth be told, none of us are all that wonderful. In the end, we don't mourn people because they're good, Kate. We mourn them because they're *ours*. Our friend, our husband, our mother."

"Bittersweet," I smiled, holding out the bag of chocolates to her.

Then, in the wonderful waning minutes of our visit, Miriam and I took turns unwrapping Sterling chocolates and popping them into each other's mouth. Like two girls at a sleepover, we talked of my new job, my new husband, and the lovely less-than-perfect futures that lay before us.

An Un-Fairy Tale

by J. Michael Squatrito, Jr.

Pain. My shoulder's shattered. A deep, stabbing ache in my side. The dome light's on, the horn blaring in an otherwise silent forest setting. Blood. My head's pounding, my forehead's warm. The airbag's pressed against my chest, the windshield's smashed, there's a pungent smell of fuel, and the hiss of steam. What happened? A deer. In the middle of the road. I swerve, going too fast, blow through the guard-rail. A fucking deer. Rolling down the embankment, two, three times. The car settles on its punctured wheels. Trees weep with fresh wounds, their limbs twisted and torn, bark scraped from their trunks.

I look to my right. My wife, the airbag pinning her, blonde hair stained red, not moving. Is she breathing? I lean over to investigate but sharp pains shoot from my shoulder and deep within my abdomen. I gasp. I try again. The pain almost knocks me out cold. I'm still secured to my seat, the seatbelt doing its job. I must get to her. I unclip the buckle from its captor, my body's free. Pivoting to my left, I fumble for the door handle. More agony. Excruciating, but she needs me. I summon my inner strength, push away the pain, flip the latch, and open the door.

I'm outside the car. I hear voices above, people shouting from the road. Red and blue flashes, screeching tires. I lumber around the car and open the passenger side door. She's not moving. Her petite body lies motionless. I know every inch of that body, having been one flesh count-less times. My wife, my lover, my soulmate, the mother of our babies.

Our babies! I squint into the backseat. Empty car seats. They're safe at home with Grammy and Pops. It's date night. The deer. *The fucking deer!* I need to save her, to look into her blue eyes again. Pain! I can hardly stand. I lean closer, I can't see her chest rising. I place my ear next to her mouth. I feel shallow breaths! The whir of helicopter blades pierce the serene landscape. A focused spotlight shines from above. A point of light. Don't go to that light! It's the wrong one!

I strain to see her beautiful face, assess her wounds. A gash on her forehead, warm blood, trickling down her cheek. Tears form in my eyes and roll down my face. I must save her, get her to see her babies one more time. She lies so still, a princess awaiting her prince. I lean even closer and press my lips to hers. Prince Charming has arrived. I taste her blood - or is that mine? My head's swooning, the pain almost succeeds in overtaking my adrenalin rush. I remove my lips. She stirs. Jesus, you've saved so many other unworthy souls, save hers! Take me, let her live to see her children, she doesn't deserve this. I hope my prayer reaches my savior. My faith says it will.

Her eyes flutter, then open. Indigo pools widen as she begins to fathom her situation. Tears flow as the pain sets in. She's alive!

"Harrison?" she says through sobs.

"Tara."

Thrashing from the embankment, the hovering chopper, the first responders rushing to the scene. I drop to one knee, exhausted, my damaged shoulder screams with anguish, my side's in agony. My head swoons. Shards of flashlight beams flood the area. A hand on my good shoulder, a paramedic has arrived. She's going to make it! Then, all goes black.

I Know His Name

by Theresa Schimmel

Days pile upon days
Pain erases their beginnings
And their endings
I no longer measure time
But wallow in despair

Endless appointments
Made and kept
Specialists of every kind
I keep on seeking
Without answer

Now, lying on white paper
Crinkling under me
I stare at the wall
With framed diplomas
And wait once more

Muted voices in the hall
Whispering what I do not know
I hear them
As they enter
Asking questions they have asked before

A cold swab of alcohol
A needle pierces my skin
I feel the liquid
Passing into my veins
And lie here mesmerized

White smocked, he enters
Reaching for my hand
His caring eyes meet mine
I exhale in relief
For I know his name;
His name is hope.

The Barber

By David Boiani

Grant Harding pulls his topcoat tight around his waist as the bitter New York winds pick up, sending a chill throughout his body. *Two more years*, he thinks as he steps around some debris dropped on the cement sidewalk. *Definitely coastal, and south. Maybe Florida, but it's so cliché. Cali? San Diego, maybe.* Retirement was in his immediate future, but what part of the country to grow old in always perplexed him. *Maybe I should stay on the East Coast, it's where I've spent most of my life. The Carolinas?* A rogue gust of wind nearly knocks him over as he strolls past a coffee shop and turns down a short alleyway off Park Avenue. Up ahead on the left side of the alley flashes a red, white, and blue pole, indicating the barber's shop which his lifelong friend, Anthony Bellini, had suggested. He and Anthony had been best friends throughout school, starting in kindergarten and lasting into their professional careers as detectives for the New York Police Department. Grant pauses at the entrance and glances up at the neon sign above which reads, 'The Hope Springs Eternal Barbieri.' *Odd name for a barbershop*, he thinks as he pulls his eyes from the glow of the neon and enters.

The place is small, with an old-school barbershop look. The floors are planks of bare wood and the ceiling is constructed of old plaster. Grant could just imagine workers applying it in globs by hand some years ago. In the front there is a lone, small desk with a cash box on it. There are three black chairs lined up facing a large mirror and a counter made of antique red brick. What strikes his senses the most, however, is the scent, a spicy aroma of bay rum combined with the earthy scent of vetiver. He closes his eyes and inhales deeply, enjoying the pleasant smell to its fullest. When he opens them, a small elderly man stands in front of him, seemingly appearing out of thin air.

"Greetingz, my friend. What iz your name?"

Grant jumps back a bit and fights to regain his senses.

"Oh, zorry. Did not mean to ztartle you."

"No, it's my fault. Daydreaming instead of paying attention."

"Ah, zere iz nothing wrong with a little dream every now and zen. I'm Guiseppe, ze barber." Guiseppe holds out his hand and Grant accepts the gesture.

"Nice to meet you, Guiseppe, my name is Grant. My friend Anthony Bellini recommended you."

"Ah, yes. Anfony iz a long-time coztumer of mine. He iz a wonderful fellow. Pleaze, haz a zeat," he says as he waves his short, thin arm toward the first of the three chairs. After Grant sits, the old man places a black apron on him and ties it around his neck.

"How do you two know each ozer?"

"We work together."

"Ahhh, you iz a detective?"

"I am. Tony and I were partners on the street."

"And how didz my name come up?"

Grant leans back in the chair and thinks about how the barber's shop actually came up in conversation. "You know, it's strange, we were discussing our careers, kinda like an overview of our lives, the wonderful memories but also the regrets. Next thing I know he was writing the name of your shop on a piece of paper."

"I zee, and how would you like ze hair cut?"

"Clean it up, a good trim,"

"Of courze."

Guiseppe goes to work and Grant's amazed at how skilled the old man is. The scissors seem to be an extension of his hands and fingers, like the blades just move naturally, bending to his will. Grant catches an angle of the old man through the mirror as Guiseppe trims the back and he swears the scissors are floating in air, an inch from the man's fingertips.

"You have nize texture to ze hair. Thick, but silky. Good for ze styling. Zo, what do ze regret?"

"Pardon?"

"About ze life. What do ze regret?"

"If only I could count. Life can be brutal. I wouldn't want to depress you with the details."

"Guiseppe no get deprezzed. Life iz to be lived to ze fullest. Try me, maybe I help."

Grant takes a deep breath. He never discusses police work with anyone outside the department. However, something about this funny little man soothes him and he decides to open up.

"A while back, before we were detectives, Tony and I received a call about a domestic disturbance. We pull up to this house off Amsterdam Avenue. Out in front on the street is this kid, maybe eighteen, waving a knife around while a young woman, his girlfriend, stands by helplessly as he berates her. We jump out and I pull my Glock and aim it at him. We collectively try to calm him down and stop him from doing something violent. He's still far enough away from the girl that I just keep my gun trained on him, with no thought of actually using it. Suddenly, he reached into his pants pocket and I instinctively pull the trigger." Grant pauses as he feels the emotion rise up. Regret, fear, grief, and confusion all combine to create one horrible feeling which overtakes him. Guiseppe feels the tension of his customer and pauses with the scissors to give Grant a moment to regain his composure.

Guiseppe only listens and continues the cut, bringing Grant's sides tight to the ears.

"His name was Tobias Williams. He was seventeen. Just a kid. He'd heard a rumor that his girlfriend had cheated on him with his best friend. What he had in his pocket was a diamond ring he had purchased for her. He was going to propose on her birthday, which was just two days away. He died instantly. There isn't a day goes by that I don't relive it and regret it. I was found innocent of any wrongdoing. My wife and child received death threats, my house was vandalized multiple times, yet still it was never enough for me to feel anything other than regret. Regret that I took a life before it had a chance to begin."

"I'm zorry for the grief ziz haz brought to you. May I azk, how is your family?"

"My wife and I got divorced. She said I changed after the incident. Said that I'd grown distant, somber. She said at the end she didn't even know who I was anymore. My son is a man now with his own family. I'm not sure he ever really forgave me for what my actions put him through as a child. It was rough on him. He was called everything from the son of a bad cop to the spawn of a murderer. He has two children of his own now. I don't see him or his family much. Only holidays and even those times have a film of coldness covering them like we really don't know each other. I think he wonders about me, about what really happened and why."

"I understand. Pleaze if you may, tilt you head down juz a bit in de front."

Grant does as instructed, closing his eyes and bowing his head.

"Now, juz relax."

Grant takes a deep breath, releasing some pent-up stress.

"Zats it, let everzing go."

Grant feels the old man's hands on the back of his head as they slowly move around the sides, stopping at his temples.

"Close ze eyez and calm ze nerves. I'll take you on a zmall journey inside your own mind."

Grant feels his pulse slow and his body soften as Guiseppe's fingertips gently massage his temples.

"I'll take you back in time to zow you a world that would have been if not for you."

Grant sees a pale, white fog inside his head. There's something bright up ahead and as the fog slowly clears, a scene takes place in his mind. There's a young man standing over a pregnant woman. He screams accusations of deception and unfaithfulness. She pleads and tries to protect her belly as her furious lover punches her on the chin sending her sprawling on the floor. He then reaches into his pocket and slowly, steadily raises an object toward her as she cries out in fear. He levels the revolver and pulls the trigger, sending the bullet into the forehead of the helpless woman. She is motionless and the man puts another into her stomach. His face seems familiar to Grant. The vision becomes clearer and there's no mistaking the face. The murderer is Tobias Williams.

Grant wakes abruptly and feels sweat pour from his forehead. He sits straight up, knocking the old man's hands from his head.

"What? What the hell was that!?" he pleads emphatically.

"Zat iz vat would've happened if he had lived. Zay would've married, ze would've had their child, and he would've killed zem both."

"How the hell would you know that? What did you do to me?"

"Relax, Mr. Harding, I'm ze friend. I only here to help you."

"How do you know my name?"

"I know lotz of zings. I'm what you would zay, magical. Ze truz iz you saved zat girl. Ze never cheated on him. Ze young man had problemz which were bound to come out zooner or later. Mr. Harding, you zaved her and her unborn child."

"What? She was pregnant?"

"Yez. Two montz."

"Was it…his?"

"Yez, it waz. Zo, you zee, zometimez what we zink iz a mistake, turnz out to be a blezzing. That girl iz alive today with a loving husband and zon, all because of you."

Even though he finds it hard to believe, Grant feels relief knowing how things turned out. Somewhere deep inside, instinctually, he knows it's true. He settles back in the chair and a feeling of relief rushes over him. He lays his head back and the old man places his fingers on his temples again.

"Zeer iz zomezing elze I need to zhow you. Juzt relax Mr. Harding."

Grant feels the magical fingertips massage the sides of his head as he closes his eyes and sees a pale, white fog in his mind. A piercing light comes into focus as the fog thins, revealing a handsome man lying in bed with a beautiful woman.

"What time is he coming for dinner tomorrow?"

"I told him to be here by noon. Will the turkey be ready by then??"

"Sure, or shortly after. So, Gavin, what happened between you two? I mean, it's strange we only see him on Thanksgiving and Christmas."

Gavin's face shows the pain that had accumulated over the years.

"I don't know. We had an incident when I was a child, I blamed him for something without knowing any better and we just grew apart. He shut down and became distant. It was like we didn't really know each other anymore and it just grew worse over the years."

The woman wraps her arms around him.

"Aw, I'm sorry, babe."

"The worst part is, I don't blame him for anything. He did what he had to do and it's taken me a while to realize that. I still love him, I always have. He's my father."

"Why don't you tell him that?"

Gavin shakes his head and stares at the ceiling.

"I don't know."

Grant wakes from the dream and looks into the mirror at the old man standing behind him.

"That was my son."

"Yez, Mr. Harding. This conversation actually took place a few yearz ago on the night before Thankzgiving."

"So, he doesn't hate me?"

"On ze contrary, he lovez and mizzez you very much."

Grant glances at himself as a few tears fall from his eyes. He's so consumed with the visions he hadn't noticed his hair was done. Guiseppe stands to the side, holding the apron he'd removed from his customer's torso.

"You like, yez?"

"Looks great, thank you."

Grant rises and walks over to the small desk.

"What do I owe you?"

"Oh no, first timerz are on ze house, my friend."

Grant starts to argue but knows by the look on Guiseppe's face it is of no use.

"So, how did you do that?"

"Zometimes people need a bit of magic in zeir lives, no? You have a long time left on ze earth. The only zing I ask from you iz you make zings right. Now you know ze truz, don't wazte it."

Grant reaches out and offers his hand, which the man accepts.

"Look, I want to thank you. You don't know what a difference this makes in my life."

"Ah, but I do. It iz why I accepted you az a coztumer."

"Goodbye, friend."

Grant turns and walks through the door. The snow had picked up and he enters a winter wonderland, covering the greatest city in the world. Grant feels like his feet aren't touching the ground, as if he's gliding over the magical white powder. His thoughts turn to Guiseppe, Tobias Williams, and his own son. He stops at a bench and sits as the snow continues to accumulate around him. Grant reaches into his pocket for his cell, goes into his contacts and taps on his son's picture. He takes a deep breath, settles himself then types...

Hi, son. I don't know or understand where we went wrong but I miss you and my grandchildren. Can we meet up for a coffee and talk?

He presses send, sits back and waits as the following two minutes seem like an eternity. Suddenly his phone vibrates. He looks down and there is a message from his son.

Sure, Dad, I'd like that. Tomorrow, noon?

Grant smiles and places his cell back in his pocket and rises. Suddenly, an odd feeling comes over him. He turns on his heels, heads back toward the coffee shop and turns down Guiseppe's alleyway. At the end, the spot where the barbershop was ten minutes prior, there's only a brick wall. No red, white, and blue barber pole, no neon light, no old, magical barber. He stands there for a minute just staring at the wall until finally he takes out his cell and dials the number for Anthony, who picks up on the second ring.

"Hello?"

Grant pauses, then responds.

"Thank you, my friend."

"You're welcome."

Grant hangs up and turns back toward Park Avenue with a feeling of absolution in his soul. He shuffles through the snow past the coffee shop, headed home to begin his new life.

Until Death Do Us Part

by Judith Boss

On September 17th the authorities at the Seabrook Nuclear Power Plant received an urgent call. The caller claimed to have overheard a phone call in a parking lot in downtown Boston about a plot to blow up the power plant. The nearby Coast Guard station was notified. They immediately dispatched a helicopter to survey the area around the plant.

A flock of Canada geese took to the air, protesting noisily as a low-flying helicopter appeared over the horizon. The helicopter zig-zagged across the marsh, its nose lowered like a hound sniffing out prey, then turned and headed in the direction of the nuclear power plant.

Joanne shielded her eyes and looked out across the saltmarsh at the retreating helicopter. The sweet scent of marsh grass filled the air. Her weathered clapboard cottage, situated on a spit of land that jutted out into the marsh, sat just outside the half-mile security zone for the nuclear plant.

She rubbed her arms and thought back to her freshman year at Boston University. It had been the spring of 1977, over 35 years ago, when the nuclear power plant was still under construction. She had been one of more than 1,000 protestors arrested with the Clamshell Alliance and jailed for criminal trespass. She frowned. How naïve she had been back then.

Now that she was more mature, she had come to accept nuclear power as the lesser of two evils because it did not produce greenhouse emissions. Then again, there were other problems. Just a few months ago, she had signed a petition at the local library to have the plant closed down because of cracks in the concrete containment dome. Even the Nuclear Regulatory Commission had expressed concern about relicensing the plant. She pushed back a stray lock of frizzy brown hair. She didn't want any trouble. Maybe she shouldn't have signed that petition.

Raising her binoculars, she scanned the power plant. She didn't notice anything unusual. But was hard to tell with the tall marsh grass and sedges blocking her view.

She set the binoculars down and glanced at the birding scope tucked under the eaves of her cottage. The scope belonged to Sameer. She had first met Sameer al-Shirazi a few weeks ago. He had set up his birding scope not far from her cottage. The tidal marsh, which was punctuated by two narrow rivers, was a favorite birding spot for birdwatchers.

Gathering her courage, Joanne had approached him. He told her he was observing the osprey nest near the power plant. He stepped aside to let her look through the scope. It was a Swarovski Scope with an attached camera—the Cadillac of scopes, he told her. Sure enough, there were three osprey fledglings in the nest.

They chatted for a few minutes. He asked her if it worried her living so close to a nuclear power plant.

She shrugged. "No, not really." She didn't want to appear like some scared and vulnerable woman living alone.

He nodded and went back to his bird watching.

"Except," she added, hoping to keep the conversation going, "I was once part of a protest at the plant—but that was a long time ago."

He straightened up and looked at her. "Oh? Tell me about it."

"Well, I . . ." She paused. It wasn't like she was some sort of antinuclear crackpot who wanted to return to the Stone Age.

"Were you part of the Clamshell Alliance protest?" he had asked.

She hesitated, then told him about her part in the protest and her subsequent "arrest."

"Good for you," he replied. "It takes a lot of courage to take a stand like that."

Joanne blushed. "If you're interested in learning more about ospreys," she said, hoping to change the subject, "the local library has a great collection of natural history books." She paused then added, "I go to there every Monday morning to read the newspapers and latest magazines."

* * *

A pair of herring gulls flew overhead softly mewling, rousing Joanne from her reverie. She glanced in the direction of the power plant. The helicopter was preparing for a landing.

She sat forward and ran a finger over the soft petals of one of the neatly arranged wildflowers sitting in a vase on the patio table. Sameer. He had charisma, a power over her as strong and bright as the current than ran from the nuclear power plant to light up the homes in the area. With his tall, lean body, clear blue eyes and dark wavy hair, he reminded her of that

actor, Henry Cavill, who played Superman. He was probably several years younger. But what is age? Just a number. He looked about as Arab as Superman, too. She squirmed in her chair and made a mental note to ask him about his name—if the opportunity arose.

Closing her eyes, she sank back and reminisced about their first meeting at the library, a wooden building situated on a hill overlooking the harbor. It was the following Monday. She had just sat down with her pile of magazines at a table in the basement of the library when she noticed Sameer trying to log on to one of the public computers.

Gathering her courage, she walked over to him.

"You need a library card to log on," she said, as though it were her fault.

"Oh, I didn't realize," he replied, grinning sheepishly. "I just wanted to look up some information on the ospreys. But since I don't have a library card with me, I guess I'll have to come back later." He stood.

"Here." Joanne pulled out her library card and handed it to him. "You can use mine. Keep it as long as you need."

To thank her, he had invited her for dinner at Captain Jack's Seafood Restaurant in nearby Hampton Beach.

As they ate, he told her he was a scientist at MIT in the nuclear science and computer-engineering program.

"I'm afraid I'm a bit of a dinosaur when it comes to technology," Joanne had replied. "I have an old laptop computer at home but I haven't used it in a while. I think it has a virus or something."

"Maybe I could take a look at it," Sameer offered.

A young man wearing a black vest came over to clear away their salad plates.

"So, tell me more about your work," Joanne said once the waiter had left.

"I'm interested in how nuclear energy can be used to benefit society." Sameer leaned forward and placed his arms on the table. "But nuclear energy, as I'm sure you know, is a double-edged sword. As I'm sure you know, there is always the possibility of radiation leaks as well as the threat of someone using the technology to produce nuclear weapons. That's why safety is my number one concern."

"Mine too," Joanne said. "That's why I joined that protest back in college."

"You're a true jihadist." He reached out and placed his hand on hers.

She laughed nervously. "I don't think so. Anyway, I'm opposed to violence."

"You know the real meaning of Jihad is a struggle for the way of God or righteousness," he said. "It can take the form of a nonviolent protest."

Of course, she knew that from her college political science course. He must think her a real dolt. She sighed.

"Hey, I had a dog named Jihad once," Sameer said, with a twinkle in his eye. "He was so into nonviolence he would only eat vegetarian dog food."

Joanne smiled. He certainly knew how to put her at ease.

The waiter returned with two plates of Maine baked crab and bacon stuffed lobster tails. Joanne glanced up at a couple walking by: a dark-haired beauty in a colorful shimmering sarong and an older man with a white embroidered tunic, probably tourists from India or Pakistan. She looked down at her own clothes: a calf-length khaki skirt and baggy green cotton sweater to conceal her bulge. She sucked in her stomach and made a silent pledge to lose ten pounds.

"A penny for your thoughts," Sameer said, picking up his lobster fork.

"I was just wondering," Joanne said, glancing at the couple who were now seated at a nearby table. "Where are you from originally?"

Sameer looked at her blankly.

"What I mean is, you don't have an accent or . . ."

He laughed. "Ah, you mean the foreign-sounding name Sameer al-Shirazi."

Joanne looked down at her hands. She felt like a bigot; why did she assume he was not born in America? Stupid. That's what she was.

Sameer leaned forward and touched her hand. "It's okay," he said softly. "I wasn't laughing at you."

Joanne blushed.

"My family?" He thought for a moment then replied, "Well, let's see. My father was from Saudi Arabia. My parents met when he was on sabbatical at UCLA. My mother was his graduate student. I was born and raised in California."

"Where are your parents now?"

He blotted his mouth with his napkin. "They died a few years ago," he said. "An automobile accident."

"Oh, I'm so sorry."

"How about you?" he asked. "Do you have family nearby?"

"I have a younger brother Derek who lives in Rhode Island."

"Do you see him often?"

"Not that often. He's a professor at the University of Rhode Island."

"How about friends? Any close friends?" Sameer asked.

Joanne shifted in her seat. "Not really." Come to think of it, she hadn't made any friends here in New Hampshire except maybe Sheila, who volunteered on and off at the library. But that was a casual friendship at best. Joanne sighed. Sameer probably thought her some lonely spinster.

But instead he seemed pleased.

"I don't have many friends, either," he said, pulling out his wallet. He took out a credit card but then quickly put it back, but not before Joanne noticed the name "Peter" something on the card. She looked away. She didn't want to appear nosy. Maybe it was a card he had found and was going to return.

"Can I help pay?" she asked, reaching for her purse.

"No, it's my treat," he said, placing six twenty-dollar bills on the table. He leaned forward and gently brushed a stray hair off her forehead.

Joanne smiled and thought of the wedding picture of her parents on the stone mantle over the fireplace in her cottage. Sameer was not at all like her father. Her father had been a loser—a swindler—an insurance salesman who preyed on grieving and lonely widows.

She took a deep breath. "Thank you. The dinner was lovely." She hesitated then added, "Maybe you could come over to my house for dinner sometime."

"I'd love to," he replied, standing up and offering her his arm.

"How about next Friday?"

* * *

Sameer arrived early on Friday and spent the first twenty minutes working on her computer. "Do you have email?" he called from the living room.

"I have Gmail," Joanne replied. "My brother set it up so I could stay in touch with the world— as he puts it." She laughed and rolled her eyes. She prided herself on her simple life. "But I haven't used it for the past few weeks. Like I said, I haven't been able to get onto the computer."

As she headed to the kitchen, she heard the desk drawer open and heard what sounded like a click.

"Do you need something?" she called from the kitchen.

"Um, just looking for a paper clip," he called back.

"They're in the bottom right drawer."

"Thanks. Just give me a more few minutes."

She stayed out of the way, fussing about putting together a plate of appetizers: lemon tarragon shrimp, assorted olives, and pita chips with feta cheese. For dinner she had prepared lamb kasha with rice and homemade tomato sauce, a recipe she had found at the library in a book on *Saudi Arabian Cuisine*.

"Do you mind if I take your computer to a colleague at MIT?" Sameer called. "He should be able to figure out what is wrong. I'll have it back to you by next week."

"That would be fine."

"I'll take it out to my car right now, so I don't forget it. Speaking of forgetting, I still have your library card. But I left it home."

"Keep it as long as you need," she said.

They spent the rest of the afternoon watching birds through his scope: black ducks, mallards, mergansers, marsh hawks, redwing blackbirds, and sandpipers.

"Is this yours?" he asked, pointing to the canoe pulled up along the grassy shore in the little cove near her house.

"Yes, it came with the cottage."

"Do you take it out often?"

"Not a lot," she said. "Although when I first moved here, I accidently paddled out into the forbidden zone around the nuclear plant and got chewed out by the guards."

Sameer threw his head back and laughed. "I can't believe it! This is too perfect."

Joanne flushed and looked away. She felt foolish for having done something so stupid.

"What I mean," he said, spreading out his hands a gesture of apology, "is we have so much in common. Not only do we both enjoy birding, I'm an avid canoeist as well." He squatted down and ran his hand across the rim of the canoe. "An Old Town square stern canoe," he said. He looked up at her. "Did it by any chance come with a motor mount?"

She thought for a moment. "There's a small motor in the shed. It was there when I moved here. I'll show you."

He stood up and wiped his hands on his jeans. "Okay. But, first, let me get a picture of you in front of the canoe. Wait there, my cell phone is in the car."

When he returned, he was holding a wicker picnic basket. "I thought we could use a few props," he said. "I just happened to have this basket in my car."

"Props?"

"Yes." He flashed a smile. "I hear we're going to have an especially high tide next week — perfect for a romantic sunset canoe trip and picnic."

She blushed. *Did he say romantic?*

Their hands brushed as he passed her the picnic basket.

Joanne almost swooned. Life suddenly seemed so perfect.

Following dinner, they retired to the living room area. Joanne lit a Firelog in the fireplace, and settled back on the floral couch across from the fireplace with a glass of pinot noir.

"I see you like old movies," Sameer said, thumbing through her neatly organized DVD collection in the bookcase beside the fireplace.

"I do—especially ones set in foreign countries."

"If you could travel anywhere, somewhere exotic, where would it be?" he asked, taking a seat in the armchair next to the bookcase.

She thought for a moment. "Well, I've always wanted to see Morocco. *Casablanca* is one of my all-time favorite movies."

He leaned over and pulled out a DVD. "Ah, *Casablanca.* A classic, and one of my favorites as well."

* * *

The sound of shouting from the direction of the nuclear plant jolted Joanne back to reality. Standing, she walked over to the birding scope. Sameer had dropped by that morning to return her computer and to pack the canoe for a sunset picnic on one of the small islands that dotted the marsh.

She scanned the area in front of the nuclear plant. People were rushing about like ants. She could make out three security guards armed with high power rifles. *What was going on?* Low waves slapped at the shoreline, twisting the tall sea grass as it struggled against the rising tide.

Just then she spotted what looked like the narrow prow of a boat riding low in the water just inside the buoys that marked the half-mile "forbidden zone" around the nuclear plant. She adjusted the scope and looked again. But it had drifted out of sight. She stepped back and took a deep breath. The spicy scent of bayberry bushes hung in the air.

As she sat down, she heard a frantic cheeping. Jumping up, she peered in the direction of the sound. A cat darted out from behind a rock, a bird dangling from its mouth, and disappeared into the clumps of Shasta daisies that lined the flagstone path leading to the dock. She frowned. She disliked cats. Cute and fluffy on the outside but inside nasty beasts. Serial killers. She made a mental note to call Animal Control first thing in the morning.

As she turned back to her cottage, she noticed the canoe was missing. The slack rope that had held it swished back and forth on the rising water. Sameer had been down there earlier preparing it for their picnic. Maybe he had forgotten to retie it or the knot had worked itself loose. She stared across the marsh. Well, there was nothing she could do about it now.

She checked her watch. 5:59 PM. She glanced back at the narrow road that led up to her cottage. But the only life she spotted was a pair of seagulls fighting over a clam one of them had dropped and smashed on the rocks that littered the rutted dirt road.

She stepped into the living room and checked her watch again. Sameer had told her to call if he was more than twenty minutes late, in case he got caught up in his work and forgot the time. She had a fleeting urge to call him, but pushed it aside. She did not want to appear too anxious. Besides, he knew she was a stickler for detail and would wait until 6:20 to phone if he was late. He said that was one of the things he liked about her, her attention to detail, her discretion. Anyway, she normally did not phone men. She subscribed to the old-school etiquette where proper girls waited for the man to phone.

She glanced at the small slip of paper Sameer had left on her desk with the number on it: "92." Thirteen minutes to go before she could call.

Sitting down at her desk, she pressed the power button on her computer. The screen lit up. A white box appeared against the blue background asking for a password. It looked like Sameer had it up and running again.

She tried typing in her old password. No luck. After unsuccessfully trying some other combinations she clicked on "switch user." The screen went dark for a second then the same screen came up again.

She was about to give up when on a whim she typed in JIHAD. Eureka! She felt breathless with excitement. Of course. A lot of people used the name of a beloved pet as their password. She checked her email. The "In" and "Out" boxes were empty except for one email from Expedia.com that had arrived that morning. She opened it. It was a confirmation in her name for an airplane ticket from Boston to Casablanca. The last four numbers of the credit card used matched those of the MasterCard she kept in her desk drawer. How bizarre. She hadn't used that credit card in months. Was this some sort of scammer trying to trick her into confirming the purchase?

Her phone rang. She grabbed it, hoping it was Sameer.

It was Sheila, her friend from the library.

"I was at the library sorting books in the back room when I overheard a phone call," Sheila said in a voice barely above a whisper. "I phoned you as soon as I could."

"Oh? What was the call about?"

"It was about you. They were asking about your Internet use at the library."

"Who's *they*?"

"Homeland Security. They said you were using the Internet to check out sites on building homemade nuclear bombs."

"Well, that's ridiculous. Is this some kind of a joke?"

"That was my first reaction," Sheila said. "That it was a joke. But they were serious as far as I could tell. I mean, you of all people, a terrorist? How crazy can you get?"

Joanne shook her head. "It was probably one of those Travelocity-type sites I was looking at to book a flight to Washington next spring to see the cherry blossoms. They probably thought I was going to blow up the White House or something stupid like that."

Sheila snorted, "A person can't do anything nowadays without Big Brother watching."

"I agree. Honestly, what has this world come to?"

Joanne glanced out the window as she hung up the phone. The Coast Guard helicopter was hovering in the air above the nuclear power plant. A steady stream of cars poured out the main gate. It must be a shift change, she thought.

She checked her watch. 6:16. She picked up the cell phone and went back outside. Peering through the scope, she spotted the boat she had seen earlier drifting toward the nuclear plant. The setting sun glinted off the aluminum prow. It looked like her wayward canoe. It was floating low in the water, as though it was carrying a heavy load.

Two men in khaki security uniforms stepped into the water and began dragging the canoe to the shore beside the power plant. They lifted the tarp and looked under it.

Suddenly a deafening blare shattered the air as sirens went off.

The helicopter took a sharp turn and began heading in her direction.

Joanne covered her ears. *What now? Another evacuation drill?* She didn't remember any announcement of a practice drill. She wondered where Sameer was. She checked the time again. Almost 6:19. She punched in the number "92." One more minute.

The roar of the helicopter blades stirred up the water as it dipped down and drew nearer. A great blue heron lifted up and flew off, its long legs trailing behind it, as the helicopter thundered overhead, pushing the water below outward in jagged ripples.

Maybe they had recognized her canoe and were coming to arrest her for some silly charge like not properly securing your canoe.

A man holding a large rifle leaned out the door of the helicopter and yelled, "Drop the . . ."

The whirr of the blades drowned out the rest of his sentence.

"I can't hear you," Joanne shouted back.

He raised his rifle and pointed it at her.

Another man, also armed, began descending a rope ladder that dangled from the helicopter.

My, aren't they being just a bit melodramatic, Joanne thought. "Okay, okay, I just have to make a quick call first," she shouted back as she pressed the "send" button.

A blinding flash lit up the sky.

The helicopter disappeared in a burst of searing white light. Joanne gasped as a blast of hot wind blew through her, incinerating her.

* * *

Two men in white hazmat suits sifted through the rubble where Joanne's cottage once stood. All that remained was the charred stone fireplace.

Lieutenant Cavallo of the U.S. Coast Guard poked at a piece of twisted metal with his boot. "What cause could be so important that this Joanne Dubois lady would blow herself up for it?"

Ross Macklin of Homeland Security stared off in the direction of the damaged nuclear plant. "Anti-American sentiments. She's been on our radar ever since being arrested at the Seabrook protests in 1977." He paused and checked the air contamination monitoring unit for radiation level.

"Were you able to get her email records?" Lieutenant Cavallo asked.

"Yes. Fortunately, Google saves all the emails now in case we need to access them."

"What did you learn?"

"She had sent her brother an email several days ago," Macklin replied, pulling a slip of paper from his pocket. "It was sent last week and said: 'Met this wonderful man Sameer al-Shirazi. I'm in love. Thinking of converting to Islam.' That email was followed by another one to her brother three days later, which would put it two days before the incident. It said: 'What a *blast*. I can't wait to see what's going to happen.' She deleted the emails after sending them, but of course we were able to retrieve them."

"Any chance someone else sent them using her email account?" Cavallo asked. He stooped over and picked up a half-melted DVD disc.

Macklin tucked the paper back into his pocket. "We checked her home phone records," he said. "There were no calls to anyone named 'Sameer.' But she had placed a call to a Sheila Connors the week before the incident. Connors volunteers on and off at the same local library where Dubois apparently was looking up websites on how to make nuclear weapons."

Cavallo shook his head. "I guess she thought we couldn't trace her if she used a library computer."

"Who knows what she was thinking," Macklin said. "We questioned Connors and she told us that Joanne Dubois had told her that she had met a wonderful man who worked at MIT and was named . . ."

"Sameer?"

"You guessed it. Connors said neither she nor any of the other librarians remember seeing him, or anyone resembling him, at the library, even though Dubois had told her she met with him there more than once."

Cavallo frowned as he checked his notes, "That's odd," he said, "given that old man Sameer was handicapped and would need the special elevator to get down to the computers."

Macklin shrugged. "Sneaky bastards, those Arabs—who knows how the old man got in there. In any case, unfortunately, we didn't get to Dubois in time to prevent her from setting off the nuclear device with a cell phone."

"I hear the bomb was transported to the site in a canoe."

Macklin nodded. "That's right. It was a small suitcase nuclear device with less than a mile range. But at least we were able to evacuate almost all the people from the power plant and warn the nearby residents of the area before it went off. It blew out the windows of some of the homes in town but there were only minor injuries."

"How did they know to evacuate?"

"An anonymous phone call came in about half an hour before the blast saying, 'Bomb!' Then the caller hung up."

"Were you able to trace the call?" Cavallo asked.

"Unfortunately no. It was from something like one of those prepaid Tracfones you get at Walmart. All we know is that it was sent from the downtown Boston area, not far from the MIT campus."

"MIT? Isn't that where you said this Sameer al-Shirazi guy works?"

"It is. Turns out, he's an 84-year-old visiting professor emeritus at MIT from the nuclear engineering program at the King Saud University in Riyadh, Saudi Arabia. He's pretty frail, has incurable stomach cancer, is in a wheelchair. He's also a Sunni Muslim."

Cavallo snorted. "I wouldn't trust a Muslim any farther than I could throw a cat."

Macklin shook his head. "I could not agree more. We found photos of the power station on his work computer—lots of them—sent from Joanne Dubois's computer. You could see every crack and fissure in the concrete dome." He pointed a gloved hand in the direction of the marsh. We figure that the photos were taken from the shore over there just beyond her property. There was also a photo in an email to him of her standing beside the canoe with what looked like the picnic basket with the bomb in it."

"How did he explain the photos?"

"The old man speaks only broken English. But he claimed he had no idea who sent the photos. Also claims he's never heard of a Joanne Dubois."

"Maybe he hasn't..." Cavallo added thoughtfully.

"We placed him under arrest this morning," Macklin said, cutting him off. "Of course, he denies everything. And there's more: We found a reservation for a plane ticket to Morocco in Dubois's email—scheduled to leave the night of the incident."

"I wonder why Casablanca?"

"For political asylum would be my guess," Macklin replied. "Morocco is one of the few countries the U.S. does not have an extradition treaty with."

Cavallo shook his head. "It's hard to believe someone so naïve could pull this off."

"You never know. It's always the ones you least suspect."

My Lover Waits

by Barbara Ann Whitman

My lover waits on foreign ground
Across the wine-dark sea
I know not where he lays his head
When he dreams of me

Yet, I think I know his voice
I'd recognize his scent
His gentle sighs have come to me
Before my sleep is spent

How I long to press my face
Against his beating heart
To feel his breath upon my cheek
Would surely be a start

A simple thing, to board a plane
Would satisfy my longing
To touch his hand and feel his gaze
And be there in the morning

But I am wise enough to fear
And so, I hesitate
So bold a move would only serve
To coax the hand of fate

Our love, ‘til now, has been so pure
Without this validation
I dread the dark reality
That comes with confirmation

My lover waits on foreign ground
And calls out “come to me”
I’m throwing caution to the wind
With hope for what will be

Two Oaks

by Abraham Simon

Two conspicuous, ancient oaks occupy portions of the front yard of Yuri's and Josie's house. The trees demarcate the boundary of the property, a site visible to anyone who wants to inspect it using Google Earth. Yuri suspects when the two trees cast their respective glances or glares up at the satellites in the sky, one remains stoic and the other grumbles. The first has droll notions about being a matinee Internet star during afternoon prime time. The second ruminates about the invasion of privacy by purveyors and buyers of real estate. But as oak trees are wont to do, in fact and in complicity, they also cast all manner of detritus on Yuri's lawn: acorns, leaves, twigs, sticks, branches, and rare colossal boughs, those unexpected widow-makers.

Nor'easters, summer squalls, windstorms, and autumn are Yuri's calls to action to clear debris deposited on his grass by the oaks. Today is no different after yesterday's gales, and all must be picked up and carted away in short order. Armed with rake and wheelbarrow, he staves off the compunction to put this work off until tomorrow and proceeds post-haste to his task. He attributes his punctiliousness, this necessity for meticulous, swift, responsive cleanups to maintain a neat yard, to his father's guidance about how to execute chores more than fifty-five years ago when Yuri was a twelve-year-old. As Yuri fills the pushcart with dead wood and restores the lawn to its typical tidiness, he regards the results of his labor with pleasure and pride. Then, in his mind's eye, he contemplates the chronic shambles of his home office, a disaster area he constitutionally sustains in such a state in perpetual rebellion against his mother.

Childish. Ridiculous, he knows. But some things, they die hard. Many things die hard.

He, Yuri's father, said *if a job is worth doing, you will find value in doing it well and on time.*

She, Yuri's mother, said *get your room cleaned up right now if you know what's good for you.*

Offspring of immigrants and children of the Great Depression, Yuri's parents were encouraged by theirs to pursue the American Dream during the country's economic struggles. But they did not know why their parents, Yuri's grandparents, chose to come to the United States. When asked about what their homes and lives were like in Europe, *they said nothing.* But they provided. They learned enough English, got jobs, worked very, very hard, always put food on the table, and were scrupulous in how they raised their children, Yuri's parents, urging them on to bigger and better.

He said *growing up, I was a roly-poly hooligan! My friends and I loved to play hooky and sneak into the movie house without paying. Or we pulled all kinds of tricks on our teachers when we did go to school!*

She said *my father and mother gave me most of what I wanted. So, when I was seven, I asked them to buy me a violin. I really wanted a clarinet but got the names mixed up and was too embarrassed to admit it. I played that violin for four years and hated every minute of it.*

Yuri wonders why his father and mother were different. What in their backgrounds made them so? He, smart, hard-working, collaborative, a joker, and the eternal optimist. She, also smart - excepting her childhood confusion about nomenclature for woodwinds and strings - also hard-working, but self-centered, fear-based, and the persistent pessimist. Perhaps it was their different experiences as they grew up? They had different parents but they, Yuri's grandparents, seemed so alike to him when he knew them as a youngster before they passed away.

Family histories were concealed and buried deep, as indiscernible to Yuri as they were to his parents. Yuri knew enough of late nineteenth and early twentieth century Eastern European history to speculate about why his grandparents were reticent about their lives there, what with war, drought, famine, pestilence, czars, and Cossacks. He knew he might uncover facts about them and his parents by purchasing one of those genetic tests. But he also realized his grandparents hoped for better lives for their children, lives that could be far less horrific than their past lives, their extinguished lives, which they chose to never divulge to them. And this deserved respect. Maybe it deserved privacy, too. Yuri was a beneficiary of his grandparents' goals and efforts that were transmitted through his parents. Shouldn't he defer to his grandparents' wishes?

Yuri's father attended college, became a geologist, and served in the U.S. Army during World War Two. Yuri's mother completed high school, got a job in a five-and-dime store, and gave dance lessons at a local studio on the side. They met after the war, married, and moved from New York to the mid-West. Their first child was born with devastating congenital defects and died seven days later.

She said *why did this horrible thing happen to me? I don't think I can go on.*

He said *why don't we try again?*

Yuri and his two older brothers were soon born in close succession. They are all alive and kicking today, sufficiently fit to manage each of their own oak trees' diverse contributions to the lawns of their respective yards. They all continue to dodge widow-makers with success, too.

The family relocated back East and Yuri grew up shadowing his brothers in all they did. Yuri made his own friends and wanted to keep up with them, too.

He said *looks like Yuri needs wheels if he wants to ride around with his chums. Time to get him a bicycle!*

She said *with training wheels so he doesn't fall and get hurt. And in another year.*

Yuri loved to wrestle with his older brothers, who were bigger and stronger and knew not to hurt him. But his encounter with a bully one day in the schoolyard after class ended was not so benevolent. Yuri returned home disappointed about the experience but flaunted his bruised eye and bloody nose as a badge of courage.

He said *I don't want you to start fights, but if the other guy takes that first punch at you, you've got every right to defend yourself. I'll show you how to put up your dukes!*

She said *you shouldn't fight at all. It's better to just run away.*

Yuri's and his brothers' religious training was perfunctory, essentially out-licensed to instructors at the local house of prayer. Yuri was dissatisfied because his unasked questions were never addressed. When he came to his parents, he realized they drew their respective spiritual perspectives from sources other than organized religion. Different sources, in fact, because their counsel was inconsistent when he queried them about his fear of death and confusion about concepts of eternity and infinity and whether or not there was an afterlife in a heaven or a hell.

He said *yes, we all die. But there is proof God exists and physics tells us about different dimensions of time and space we don't perceive. Don't worry! Everything will be okay.*

She said *I think when you die, that's it. When you're dead, you're dead.*

It's the day after another New England deluge with high winds. Yuri surveys his front yard and sees the amount of lumber liberated onto his lawn by the two oaks is less than he expected. Turning his attention to the bases of the two trees, he is reminded of their dissimilitude. The turf surrounding the base of one enjoys a surfeit of sunlight that supports a plethoric growth of grass. The ground around the other suffers from less sun exposure, and its trunk is surrounded by large patches of bare dirt laden with an assortment of medium-sized rocks, small stones, and pebbles. Yuri sits by the tree to pick up fragments of gneiss, granite, marble, schist, and other samples, the names of which he cannot recall from his father's tutoring long ago, and he collects them to drop on the rock path in his backyard. He is puzzled by how new stones appear in this patch only days after he plucks out all he can find.

Competing activities confronted Yuri when he attended high school: advanced classes, band practice, basketball, school dances, time with friends. He wanted to do everything and sought guidance about how to prioritize and balance his time.

He said *work hard, play hard* when he and Yuri plugged away together in the workshop in the garage or went one-on-one with a basketball.

She said *don't hurt yourself* as she chain-smoked her Pall Malls.

College courses challenged Yuri, but he did well. His parents helped by paying part of his tuition and he worked as a dishwasher at a restaurant to meet the rest of his expenses. With the hours spent in class, doing homework, and being on the job, there was little time for rest. Yuri sought encouragement.

He said *losing a little sleep from time to time never killed anybody. You'll be all right.*

She said *you'll catch your death of cold if you don't get to bed on time every night.*

Yuri brought Josie home to introduce her to his parents. They had dated for two years and were in love. She would agree to become his wife, now going on forty years. But back then, Yuri had not yet decided to ask her to wed.

He said *do not heed what others say. It's better to trust your instincts and your gut. But, Son, it's best to trust most what is in your own heart.*

She said *she's no good for you.*

Yuri completed graduate school and embarked on a career that required frequent domestic and international travel. He was conscientious about calling his parents every time before he boarded a plane, responsive to his mother's repeated requests he do this.

He said *enjoy the trip! Don't do anything I wouldn't do!*

She said *did you send me your itinerary? Call me as soon as you land.*

Yuri and Josie moved away, but they visited Yuri's parents several times a year. He called them at least once a week to keep in touch.

He said *you know? As you get older it seems you spend more and more time in doctors' offices. The good thing is you can find some pretty interesting magazines in the waiting room!*

She said *those doctors! They really don't know what the hell they're doing. Besides, I know my own body best.*

Yuri and Josie got new jobs in-state to be closer to both of their parents. Soon after they returned home, his father's brother died after a long illness. Yuri sat next to his father in the funeral chapel.

He said *they are dropping like flies* with a smirk and a wink.

She said *when will this service end? I need a drink.*

Yuri's father was next. He met the widow-maker though he was fit, exercised every day, and never had a serious medical problem until he developed a cough two months before. The widow-maker was not a large bough of an oak tree that fell on him but a tumor of his bronchial tree that grew inside of him. Lung cancer. As far as Yuri knew, his father never smoked a day in his life. But now this. And it had spread everywhere. The doctors said they didn't know what caused it, but Yuri was sure it was the second-hand smoke. With anger and guilt, Yuri thought it was not supposed to be his father who would have something like this happen to him.

Two weeks later, before the start of his chemo, Yuri's father got short of breath, turned blue, and was rushed to the hospital by ambulance. When Yuri, Josie, and Yuri's mother were allowed to go into the intensive care unit to visit, he was unconscious, connected to a breathing machine, and hooked up to all kinds of monitors and bags of fluid flowing through tubes into the veins of his arms.

She said *shit! Shit! SHIT!*

He said nothing.

Yuri was startled but not surprised by what his mother blurted. It was selfish, but her life was about to take a crucial turn. He did not expect his father to say anything because he was sedated, in an artificial coma, and a breathing tube was down his throat. But his silence and lack of acknowledgement, despite Yuri's, his wife's, and his mother's beseeching him to respond in some way, in any way with an unspoken signal, reminded Yuri of his grandparents. How *they said nothing* in response to questions about their past lives. Yuri wondered what his father could not and did not want to say. And would never have to say.

For the next twenty days and twenty nights, Yuri and his family came to the hospital hoping to learn of progress and praying for a miracle. For twenty days and twenty nights *he said nothing.* And on the twentieth night, the doctors advised there was no hope. They asked Yuri's mother if they could stop life support and she consented. For twenty days and twenty nights, Yuri's father died hard. His heart was the last of him to stop, only moments after the breathing machine was turned off.

Yuri opined to his mother, brothers, and Josie about his father's luck to have had good health for almost all of his seventy-six years. The planned treatment for his type of advanced cancer was not likely to appreciably increase his survival. And he would have suffered with symptoms he had never known at any time during his life. Hardly quality time.

What Yuri thought, but did not share with his family, was how wise his father was, given this opportunity of sorts, to skip town, to get out of Dodge. Could his father have known his lung cancer was not going to be a picnic? Maybe. Maybe not. Yuri also wondered if his father decided to seize the day and exit from an existence for which he no longer had any positive use. Or, more probably, to prevent prolongation of his family's agony as they observed his inevitable decline.

Yuri knew he was unkind in his thoughts. He knew he was angry with his mother, whose smoking may have contributed to his father's lung cancer, although that was never her intention. And with his father for abandoning him. His brothers lived hundreds of miles away and it would be Yuri's responsibility to provide oversight, support, and care to a being he expected to be a recalcitrant matriarch.

Yuri's mourning lasted for months. He was distraught because all he could remember about this father was the time in the hospital intensive care unit. Yuri worried about his mother. Would she sell the house and move to a smaller, more practical place? Her house – and his father's, his brothers' and his old home – was right for a family of five, but now it was all wrong, too big, and too much for his mother, an increasingly frail but immovable seventy-three-year old. Yuri recalled the last year of disagreements between his parents. Yuri's father thought it would be best to reduce, simplify, and find a different place. A home without stairs. Maybe an apartment that wouldn't take his time and effort to manage all of the repairs. She refused.

She said *Godammit! This is our home. And no one is going to take it away from me!*

Yuri rakes up the last of the leaves, finishing up near the two oaks. The day is mild and he sits by the bare patches of ground surrounding one of the trees. As he rolls a piece of quartz in the dirt, he remembers. Yuri thought his mother's opinion about the house would have to change. She did not drive and was isolated. She was mechanically inept, but her fierce independence precluded requests for help from Yuri, neighbors, or others. He understood her desire to keep everything the same, not have to change, and not give up any of her possessions. But she did need to downsize, get rid of stuff, and move. Yuri looks up at the two oaks and needs no reminder trees shed. He thinks about all of the piled-up books and papers strewn about his office. But that is deliberate. Purposeful. A memorial of sorts. Resistance to change dies hard.

Yuri worried his mother would resist. After several months of his and Josie's discussions during their visits, his brothers' supporting telephone calls, coaxing her to get out of the house on car trips to go to a movie or a restaurant, exploration of apartments in the city, and exceptionally dreary New England weather, Yuri's mother relented. Yuri volunteered to help his mother get the house organized, cleaned up, and some parts dismantled and cleared out to make it salable. His spirits were higher and fond memories of his father returned.

He said if a job is worth doing, you will find value in doing it well and on time.

She said *I can't take all of this. You must save it for me! But that damned cellar. Do what you need to do to clean it up.*

Yuri went to his mother's house on twelve consecutive weekends. He cleaned out the attics of memorabilia his mother was willing to part with as long as he stored it for her. He spackled, sanded, and painted walls needing refurbishing in several rooms. He arranged inspections of the oil burner and water heater. He repaired toilets and sinks. He mowed the grass and trimmed the shrubs. He cleaned the gutters and did patchwork and painting on the exterior. He replaced floodlights. To help decide what could be moved, he obtained the dimensions of the two-room apartment in the city that his mother selected, measured the furniture in the house, and drew up options of floor plans with different arrangements of the items she wanted to take.

Yuri's real work, an upsetting task, was the basement. Originally a playroom for his brothers and him, his father took it over for his scientific research after all the boys moved out. Yuri regarded the makeshift desk littered with pencils, pens, file cards, paper clips, rock picks, crack hammer, hand lens, calculator, and calendar, high piles of notebooks, journals, and topographical maps, wooden file cabinets, laboratory apparatus, book shelves populated by reference books, models, and several small, framed pictures, and display cases protecting the rock collections. It all seemed alive to Yuri, his father's life work. But Yuri had to turn off life support and deconstruct it all.

His father prepared instructions that helped Yuri decide what to discard and what to save. Yuri repackaged the geologic specimens for the museum. He took the papers, reference books, equipment, and apparatus to the college. After he emptied the desk, cabinets, book shelves, and display cases, Yuri was reminded of his two oaks in winter, leafless and skeletal. He took apart the furniture and the cases, more dead wood to be collected and carted away. When all was removed, Yuri painted the basement walls and floor. It looked sterile, but clean and approving, in great shape for a prospective buyer. But Yuri remembered the room's contents when he was a child and how it became the source of his father's professional inspiration.

Yuri moved his mother to her new city apartment. He knew it was best for her, but his time and work in the home of his childhood evoked memories, good and bad. Other memories returned, too: those nightmarish images of his father in the intensive care unit. Yuri wondered when he would again remember the better times with his father.

Yuri recalls when something happened. The weather was pacific. Several weeks had passed since the two oaks had discharged any litter onto his lawn. He and Josie returned home from a walk about the neighborhood and he remained outside after she reentered their house. Yuri examined the trees from afar and investigated for any low, dead branches he could remove with his pole saw. Finding none, he walked to one oak and observed its trunk surrounded by the constant green grass. Then he ambled to the other oak to sit and retrieve a few of the new stones that had surfaced in the dirt since his last visit. Yuri stowed the specimens in his pants pocket, placed both of his hands on the trunk of the tree, leaned in, touched his forehead to the bark, and listened. He recalls *it said nothing.* At first. Yuri leaned back and wondered what oak trees have to hide? He changed position and tilted sideways to the tree, his good ear close to the trunk, and he heard *why don't we try again?*

Despite her predilection for grousing, Yuri thought his mother did as well as she might, although she missed her husband. She walked where she wanted to go in the city or took the bus, shopped, befriended others in the apartment building, joined a book club, cooked for herself, and volunteered at a local school. She asked Josie or Yuri to drive her to some appointments, impatient with the unreliability of taxis in that era before Uber and Lyft might have provided more prompt service.

She said *nothing ever goes the way I want.*

Yuri cannot pinpoint when he and Josie noticed his mother's carping, unhappiness, and self-centeredness increased, probably incited by her cognitive decline. In retrospect, Yuri thought her dementia started within a couple of years of her move to the city. But the changing penmanship was attributed to her hand arthritis. Yuri overlooked the word substitutions and discontinuity of thoughts because he could connect the dots when he spoke with her. She was increasingly reluctant to leave her apartment without Yuri's or Josie's company because of her unsteadiness, vertigo, and worsening vision, problems for which she refused medical attention.

She said *I know my body best. I'm getting old. And anything those damned doctors do gives me a reaction.*

Changes in living arrangements were needed, which Yuri's mother refused to consider despite his and Josie's suggestions for several years. Until she fell. She relied on a flimsy, rolling shopping cart to walk outside, pushed it into a curb she did not see as she crossed the street, collapsed the folding frame onto her wrist, and fractured it as she toppled. As casts were applied, in-apartment help was arranged, and physical therapy was conducted, she capitulated and agreed to move to an assisted living residence.

She said *this apartment was never my home. A new place will never be my home. I'm sure I'll hate it.*

He said *why don't we try again?*

Yuri and Josie tried again, and again, and again, as they researched and orchestrated three successive moves for his mother: first to assisted living, then to cognitive care, and finally to a nursing home. For each move, Yuri and Josie investigated numerous options and he felt the weight of his responsibilities for his mother. But his brothers agreed with his choices and deferred to and supported his recommendations. For each move, Yuri determined what his mother could keep and what he would store. Yet more dead wood to collect and cart away.

His mother's mental decline and physical deterioration were slow and transpired over many years. Staff at the facilities recommended the increases in care level, from assisted living to memory care to nursing home. Yuri missed his mother, albeit the more demanding of his parents but confident in her love for and interest in him. Yuri did not mind assuming financial and health care proxy responsibilities for her. But he was disturbed by the progressive and unpredictable nature of the disease process that induced her suffering. The dementia amplified his mother's fearful, self-centered nature and converted the entirety of her conversations to diatribes. The book club was useless because no one else read the book. The movies were repetitive or ones she knew she saw before. Or the staff were ignorant and could not run the movie in the first place. The thermostat didn't control the room temperature. The windows did not open or close. Something was wrong with her telephone and the television remote because she could not get them to work. The lock on her door and all of the door knobs broke. Her pens and eyeglasses were missing. People came into her room and rearranged her things or stole them.

She said *everything here is crazy! I don't know what's going on. They don't know what the hell they're doing and don't want to help me.*

Yuri showed his mother how to work the phone and remote on multiple occasions and wrote instructions in large, block letters for her to reference. He confirmed the door locks, door knobs, windows, and thermostat functioned properly and found the stolen items in drawers, under her bed, or behind the furniture. Conversations with her devolved to listening to her constant complaining but were tolerated. However, his mother expected Yuri and Josie to spend all of their time with her, and they were obliged to abruptly conclude their visits.

She said *I want to be left alone. I wish I could just die.*

One day, the nursing home staff found Yuri's mother in her bed, not breathing and without a pulse. Death from natural causes at age ninety-three. Her heart was probably last to go, as it was for his father, but her mind began its retreat many, many years before. In accordance with advance directives and her living will, resuscitation was not performed. Yuri attended to all arrangements. Keeping with his mother's wishes, only Yuri, Josie, and his brothers and their wives attended the private funeral. Yuri's mother was laid to rest next to his father.

She said no one cares. No one will come.

Yuri's father died hard for twenty days. Yuri's mother died hard for twenty years.

Yuri admires the chaos that characterizes his home office, proud of its dishevelment. Another badge of courage. This spot in his house reminds him of his father's basement and the line he always drew between his mother and himself.

He walks into the front yard towards the two oaks with two buckets, one for the small number of twigs he will find and the other for the pieces of gneiss, granite, marble, schist, quartz, and others he will discover. Yuri contemplates his parents as he sits and collects the rocks. Looking at both oaks, he speculates about how long these two trees will be around. Or Uber and Lyft. He looks to the sky and ponders the same question about Google Earth and Earth itself.

Yuri knows some say all matter – animal, vegetable, and mineral – is all energy. But whatever these are composed of, none of it can be destroyed. It lasts forever. He knows that others say everything we do or say never goes away, never disappears. It is stored and remembered somewhere in the space-time continuum of the universe or in another dimension and remains for all time. If all of it is permanent, might it also change in some ways?

Yuri muses about his mother, hoping she is at peace or will find it, as he is confident his father has. Will she and his father find their first child, their first of four boys, and reconcile the terrible tragedy that consumed the start of their lives together? Might his mother now think her misnaming a clarinet as a violin is humorous? Could she enjoy playing and mastering a stringed instrument in the hereafter? Yuri deliberates about what might have happened to that daughter of immigrants if she wasn't refused knowledge of the adversities in her family history nor denied the context for her parents' guidance. To that child of the Great Depression if she had not been inculcated in material things. And to that fear-based and prideful seven-year-old girl if she had gotten her clarinet. Would it have made a difference? Is it making a difference now?

Yuri, in his seventh decade, son of offspring of immigrants, and child of children of the Great Depression, gazes across his front yard. Around the trunk of the one oak that towers on the sunnier side of the property, the grass still grows abundant and green. Yuri rolls a nugget of marble in his hand as he sits in the dirt beside the second oak, leans his head back against the tree's bark, and closes his eyes.

Don't worry! Everything will be okay.

Sunshine Through the Darkest Cloud

by Kevin Duarte

Mary Newfield entered her apartment and tossed the keys in the bowl next to the door. She heard the patter of four paws on the hardwood floor as the other occupant of the apartment, a furry ball of energy in the form of a Bernese mountain dog she named Shandy, came careening around the corner.

Thrump. Click. Thrump-thrump.

Thrump. Click. Thrump-thrump.

Shandy came around the corner, his feet almost wiping out from under him. The collar on his neck glowed, reading signals from the dog's brain and sending them to the mechanical hind limb which managed to keep pace with his other three legs. Although the "foot" of the mechanism was covered in a poly-rubberized compound and fitted with synthetic pads, each step of the leg during a brisk canter sounded like the floor was being hit by a leather-wrapped hammer. Shandy slid to a stop just short of Mary and nuzzled Mary's leg with his huge head and wet, prying nose.

Mary knelt down and took a moment to savor the welcome distraction and properly offered her affections onto her loyal room-mate. She rubbed both sides of his head, the brown, tan, and white patches of fur flying from the effort. The mechanical leg twitched several times even though the dog was standing still, so Mary ran her hand down Shandy's neck and examined the collar, making some minor adjustments to a thin antennae, then checked the battery. She examined the thin cable that went from the collar and entered the back of Shandy's head, receiving the impulses from the dog's brain and sending them wirelessly via the collar to his cybernetic leg. Mary watched as the mechanical leg bent and twitched as if alive. A slight adjustment to the collar, and the twitching of the leg stopped. Mary could see that everything was working correctly.

"We fixed you up, right. Didn't we, boy?" Mary said as she patted Shandy on the head. "Still can't believe they were going to destroy such a big beautiful boy like yourself." She rose and started for the kitchen. "Let's get some dinner."

Shandy's head tilted and his ears raised. He burst into a manic dash to the kitchen towards his dog bowl. Mary made her way into the kitchen and down to the basement, returning with a cup full of dry dog food. Mary opened the refrigerator and pulled out an opened can of dog food. She picked up the dog's bowl, then filled it with a mix of the dry food and a half can of the wet food from the refrigerator. Shandy squirmed with anticipation as Mary lowered the bowl to the floor.

Mary smiled as Shandy began vigorously gulping his meal. She turned to the counter, and saw a number on her answering machine. She walked over and punched a button on it.

Beep.

"Hey, Mary. It's Bruce. I'm here with Mom. You might want to swing by after you get home from work. She's...let's just say she's not doing so great today."

Beep.

Mary punched another button on the device.

"*Message deleted.*"

She opened the refrigerator and returned the can of dog food, then rummaged through the shelf and found chicken, broccoli, and a container of jasmine rice. Leaning listlessly against the kitchen door, and peering at the answering machine, Mary felt her motivation to cook dulled by the content of the message, and her necessary response to it. She reached into the refrigerator and pulled out leftover Chinese food from two nights ago. She pulled the wire handle and tossed the cardboard container into the microwave, watching Shandy as he finished the last of his food, licking his bowl to ensure that he had savored every last morsel. The microwave beeped, and Shandy lifted his head and peered at Mary.

"Oh no, big boy," she exclaimed. "This is for me. We need to head out in a few."

It was a forty-five minute ride to the house Mary had grown up in. Shandy started the trip sitting in the back of Mary's SUV, but as was always the case, a few minutes into the ride he decided it would be better if he rode shotgun. Mary patted him on the head as he panted and paced, anticipating the opportunity to get out and prance in the ample yard that surrounded the large colonial-style house he was so familiar with. Mary opened the door, and Shandy bolted from the passenger's seat, heading for the house, tail spiritedly wagging as he ran. He headed toward the front door, stopping periodically to sniff near some grassy patches and next to the shrubs that adorned the front of the house. He darted around the front of the yard, distracted by all manner of birds that flew around the house. Before Mary reached the front door, it was opened by a man who exited the house. He smiled when he saw Mary approaching.

"Hi, sis," greeted the man. "I heard you pull up. Thanks for coming by." He gave Mary a hug.

"Of course," Mary replied.

"Brought your co-pilot with you?" asked Bruce, noticing Shandy rummaging through a stretch of bushes lining an area of the lawn that contained bird feeders on ornately painted wooden posts as well as several decorative stone birdbaths.

"Like he would give me any other option," laughed Mary.

Bruce laughed, then placed his fingers in his mouth and let out a whistle so loud it made Mary wince. Shandy turned at the sound, and forgoing any further olfactory investigations, launched headlong toward the front door. Bruce sidestepped the dog, managing to get hit only twice by the dog's tail as he entered the house. Mary grabbed Shandy's collar as he entered. Today, as in the recent past, he would not have free rein within the house as he had been granted in the past. The stipulations of the visit, and the condition of the occupants, deemed it necessary for the dog to be led into the study on the left. Guided sternly into the room, the dog turned back, his ears high and folded by his tilted head. Mary pointed into the room, and Shandy immediately walked to an area rug in the center of the room, paced around the edges of it in a circle three times, then plopped onto the ground with a resigned huff. Tongue hanging from his mouth, he peered back at the two as they quietly closed the door.

Mary walked down the hallway as if she were facing a fierce wind. She hesitated, reset her very footing, then with a hand on the wall for support, pulled herself deeper into the house. Bruce followed her in, casually and conveniently blocking any chance of an escape. Mary knew the look on her face relayed her anxiety like a portrait in a gallery, brightly lit and obscured by nothing. Mary turned back, peering past Bruce at the open door.

"She's in the den," Bruce announced. Mary felt that her brother was trying to distract her from a contemplated escape. The ploy worked, and she turned forward and trudged onward. The heaviness that weighed upon her about seeing her mother quickly faded when she finally saw her. Her mother sat in a huge cushioned chair next to a small, round table. The center of the table was decorated with a doily with a spiral pattern, and on top of that was a china cup filled with tea which sat next to a matching plate that held several pieces of crackers and a scattering of nuts.

Her mother was wrapped in a blanket even though it was not the least bit chilly in the house. The light on the small table illuminated her face but cast shadows that ran down the side of her body. Mary thought her mother was sleeping, but when she entered the room, her mother carefully lifted her head and stared blankly at the two people who had come to occupy the room.

"Hi, Mom," greeted Mary as she carefully approached. She crouched down in front of her and placed a hand gently on her mother's forearm. Mary felt the sinews of her mother's forearm as she gently pulled away. Mary let go of her mother, standing upright and backing slowly from the chair.

"Do I know you?" asked her mother.

Mary ran her finger down the side of her nose, slyly wiping a tear from her face. She turned to her brother, her eyes pleading to Bruce for an adequate response. He shook his head.

"She hasn't recognized me since the day before yesterday," Bruce said. "The doctor came by yesterday and said this is to be expected."

"So she's not going to get any better?" Mary dared to ask. "She's only going to get worse from here on?"

Bruce said nothing, only nodded his head.

Mary looked at her mother, taking in her features, which looked as dear to her as they had ever been. Her mother's hair, even at her age, was elegant and beautiful, and her skin reflected a graceful aging that added to her matriarchal character. She had aged well in all aspects of her body.

Her mind, however, had betrayed her.

Bruce took Mary's arm and led her to the hallway. They made their way to the kitchen and leaned against the counter, neither one wishing to take a chair.

"The doctor wants to prescribe another medication," Bruce informed Mary. "Let's hope for the best."

"Hope?" said Mary. "That's all we have to go with? Hope?" Mary shook her head, the frustration of the situation growing.

"Hope is where we find it," Bruce said. "It's not always obvious, and sometimes we really need to look for it."

"I need something a little more substantial than that," Mary retorted. She dropped her head and took a deep breath. "I'm sorry, Bruce. It's just the engineer in me. I'm not a psychiatrist like you. I need hard evidence. I need a little more than just 'hope.'"

"I understand, Mary," replied Bruce. He walked up to his sister and gave her a hug. She collapsed into his arms, tears streaming. Bruce held her, letting the emotions flow from her in silence. After several moments, Mary stood up and managed a smile for her brother.

"How's the job going?" Bruce asked. Mary knew Bruce was trying to distract her momentarily from the stress at hand, but unbeknownst to him, he had just taken her out of the frying pan and tossed her into the fire.

"It's been very stressful, lately," Mary replied. "I'm stationed at Grand Forks in North Dakota."

"When do you go back?" asked Bruce.

"Day after tomorrow," said Mary. "We are testing some new exoskeletal equipment with the grunts for the next three weeks. Our cybernetics division has become an integral part of the ground forces. I feel more like a soldier than an engineer."

"North Dakota this time of year," Bruce shook his head. "Not like being here in Oklahoma."

"Tell me about it," said Mary. "They have snow already. That's why we are there. We're trying to tweak some equipment to be more proficient in the harsher environments."

"Need me to watch Shandy?" asked Bruce.

"They're letting me take him with me," she replied. The distraction of the discussion of work fading, Mary turned and gazed through the walls into the den where her mother was sitting. She could not see her from the kitchen but was still drawn to her. "I'm going to spend time with Mom."

"The nurse is due here any minute," said Bruce. "But you can stay as long as you want."

After a plane flight into Grand Forks International Airport, Mary and Shandy drove a rental car onto the military base, checked in with security, then made their way to their quarters in the barracks. Mary was dressed in a ski jacket while Shandy pranced at her side, head lifted and nostrils expelling wisps of white vapor. He was in his element and enjoyed the brisk environment. Mary checked into the barracks, which were conveniently located next to the engineering and armament depot. Mary read the sign on the door of the depot:

"Personalized Armament and Protection Protocols."

"PAPP," as the grunts knew it. Guns and Armor. A warrior's best friend. Exoskeletons to enhance their physical abilities. Weapons to augment them. Armor to increase their longevity in battle as much as possible.

Mary knew it was a place an infantryman only wanted to visit once, because if he was coming back here, it was most likely to be fitted with a cybernetic limb like the one Shandy sported. But unlike Shandy, whose limb had been carefully removed by a veterinarian before she was handed over to Mary for reconstruction, and eventually adoption, the level of damage that a soldier encountered in battle before they were submitted for reconstruction was left only to the imagination of the engineers. Each case varied by degrees. Working with doctors and surgeons, engineers like Mary had the call on whether a soldier – a candidate for reconstruction – warranted the effort and expense required to rebuild them so they could rejoin their infantry on the front lines.

Rebuilding lambs for the slaughter.

What began as a case study in cybernetics and engineering turned into face to face meetings with the people she was sending back to combat, back to their potential doom.

This was Mary's dark cloud.

Mary made the call about who would be part of the program. She would determine whether to rebuild the soldier to a level that they had never known, or slap an inanimate prosthetic on their arm or leg and send them on their way. It was a responsibility she came to dread. When she started with the division, her job had been to design, engineer and test the cybernetic prosthetics. This was the part of the job she loved. Engineering without direct human interaction or repercussions. She would take alloy, wires, and circuits, and build something new to replace something that had been taken from someone. But as her job, as the commanding officer has stated, had evolved to a point where she needed to determine the fate of the soldier coming before her, time served and injury sustained, their eyes pleading with the hope for Mary's approval to be rebuilt to the fullest potential of both man and machine.

Pleading with hope. Always pleading. Their fate in her hands.

Mary gazed at the picture of her mother. The picture was a few years ago before she began to succumb to the ravages of the disease that stripped her of her memory, her ability to think clearly, and her personality. Her eyes were bright and her smile contagious. It was a time that Mary remembered fondly. She longed for those days again.

Mary felt helpless to bring those days back to her mother. She could rebuild the bodies of men and women, but she was helpless against the stealthy onslaught that was taking place in her own mother's mind. It was a war for which no amount of her engineering could sway the tide of battle.

Mary quickly unpacked her suitcases. Shandy sat next to the last briefcase, nose nuzzling a paper bag in the corner of the suitcase.

"Bugger," said Mary with a laugh. She opened the bag and pulled out a biscuit. "You were so good on the plane, you deserve this."

Mary tossed the treat, which Shandy caught and crunched to bits with his jaw. He dropped to the floor as he consumed the biscuit, scanning the floor with his nose looking for any pieces that might have escaped.

Mary unpacked the last of her clothes as well as a few personal items. Unlike the other times she was stationed at military bases, she felt compelled to include a picture of her mother. She carefully placed the three by five-inch picture frame next to her bed, one of a dozen army-green cots that littered the room of the barracks. Shandy hopped up on the cot and plopped down at Mary's feet just as she clicked off the light and rolled into her blankets.

"Where was the hope for my mother?" Mary thought. Mary could repair the broken bodies of soldiers she had never met before, but with all her skill and expertise, she was powerless to restore the functionality of her own mother's mind.

Mary's sleep was restless. She got up the next morning, washed up quickly, grabbed a cup of coffee for breakfast, then reported to the engineering depot for her first shift. Shandy, whose calm demeanor and canine charms instantly made him the resident therapy dog, accompanied Mary as she familiarized herself with the logistics of the engineering facility, then the two headed to the observation area to address the first few candidates. The first soldier, a woman who had been struck down by a landmine, came into the observation area. She was small, but energetic, and dressed in standard issue army fatigues.

"Morning," Mary greeted.

"Good morning," replied the soldier. She handed Mary a folder and used her hands to hoist herself onto the examining table. Even with a prosthetic limb, she was very nimble. "Oh what a beautiful dog. Is he yours?"

"He's all mine," said Mary with a smile as she began reading the file. "Katlyn Strause."

"That's me," replied Katlyn.

"Victim of an IED," Mary added. "How are you feeling?"

"I feel great," replied Katlyn.

Mary lifted her eyes from the folder without moving her head. She was trying to determine if the soldier's upbeat attitude was genuine, or whether it was manufactured to make her more appealing as a candidate for reconstruction. At that moment, she was unsure which she was witnessing.

"How long have you been in recovery?" Mary asked. The information was in the file, but she wanted to hear from the soldier herself.

"I've been in recovery for five weeks," replied Katlyn. "I was practicing with 'twig' after two."

"'Twig'?" asked Mary, amused.

Katlyn pulled off her prosthetic and slid it out of her fatigues. "Yeah, this is 'twig.'"

Mary smiled genuinely and determined that the soldier's exuberance and positive attitude was genuine. After a series of questions and a thorough examination of the injured leg, Mary gave her prognosis to the soldier. Katlyn's face became serious as she listened for her fate to be determined by a stranger she had met only a short time ago.

"I'm admitting you into the cybernetics program," said Mary. She signed a form and placed it into the folder, then handed it back to the soldier. "Congratulations. You'll be back with your unit in about three weeks."

Katlyn was exuberant, and even with the prosthetic, jumped and twirled with excitement in the examining room. She came over and hugged Mary.

"Thank you so much," said Katlyn. "You just gave me my life back."

"I gave you your military career back," said Mary. "You'd still have your life even if you left here just with 'twig.'"

Mary's words hit Katlyn hard.

"That's true," replied Katlyn. "But I still need to thank you. This is just what I was hoping for."

"Hope restored," thought Mary. For everyone else but her, and her mother.

Three more soldiers came into the observation, two of whom left disappointed. The third was a male soldier by the name of Glen Wilkes, who worked as a spotter for a sniper and lost his left arm when a mortar found its way onto the roof where he and his sniper partner were housed. The sniper suffered minimal injuries, but Wilkes, who caught most of the blast, suffered several injuries, and ended up losing his left arm at the elbow. Fortunately for him, Mary found him to be just as good a candidate as Katlyn Strause, and signed him into the program.

The examination of the four candidates took up most of the morning. Mary and Shandy headed back to the mess hall for chow, then Mary took Shandy into one of the aircraft hangers to play. He chased a ball back and forth while Mary monitored his cybernetic limb for any abnormalities. Shandy was usually a wonderful distraction and she was glad she was able to bring him with her, but her mind would not sway from thoughts of her mother.

The afternoon was much less hectic for Mary. There were only two appointments, both consisting of making adjustments to cybernetic components that had already been fitted onto soldiers who had suffered in combat. Recipients of the reconstruction program's finest cybernetic appendages, these soldiers became the prize of their respective companies, not only because of their ability to rejoin the ranks, but because of their enhanced abilities brought on by the engineering marvels that graced their bodies.

The first appointment, a woman who had received a hip-to-toe prosthetic after being injured by an artillery shell in the desert, entered the observation room for minor adjustments, and was quickly discharged. The second, a younger recruit, had both a leg and arm replaced by Mary personally several months ago, and was back after experiencing some issues with the cybernetic link to his prosthetic. He walked into the observation area and handed Mary his folder.

"I remember you," the soldier greeted. "You're Mary Newfield, right?"

Mary took the folder, then George placed himself and a small duffel bag on the examination table. With his hand, he coaxed his leg to bend to an adequate degree that would allow him to sit normally. Mary opened the folder and scanned the first page of information.

"George DuMont," Mary read aloud. "You looked familiar, but I see several soldiers, so I apologize for not remembering your name."

"No apology necessary," George commented. "I was grateful when you approved of me being in your program. It meant a lot."

"According to your folder, you are in Communications." Mary asked, "I thought this program was designed for infantry?"

"It is," replied George. "I was infantry, but they transferred me and put me in another program here as well."

"What type of program?"

"Cerebral augmentation," replied George. "They are trying to make me a better communications officer. I probably shouldn't be telling you this. It's all classified. Top Secret stuff."

"I won't tell anyone," said Mary.

Cerebral augmentation. The term piqued Mary's interest. Mary looked around before asking a follow-up question.

"What type of protocol does this new program use?" Mary asked as she walked over and removed a scanner from a drawer.

"Injections," replied George. George reached over and grabbed his duffel bag. He looked around, then unzipped the bag. He pulled out a vial and handed it to Mary. "Every twelve hours. I take one during breakfast and the other during dinner."

"What does it do?" Mary asked.

"Picks up where you leave off," replied the soldier, tapping the alloy of his leg. He pointed to his temple. "Augments the brain matter. Doctor says it builds new neurological pathways… lots of them. Made me a new man, but there was a small chance it could have killed me. I decided to take the chance and it paid off."

Mary examined the vial, then returned it to the soldier. She put the scanner on the examining table and assessed the prosthetic with her hands. She checked the connections from the leg to the cranial connector that had been surgically implanted into George when the leg and arm were installed. Like Shandy, the soldier had a thin wire with a protective coating that went from the collar into a circular patch attached to the back of his head. Mary carefully checked the wire to make sure it was secure.

"Good connection from your brain to the cranial collar," commented Mary. "That's a good sign, otherwise we'd have to reopen that skull of yours and look around."

George smiled at the jest, and Mary smiled in return.

"Have you noticed a difference since being part of that other program?" asked Mary.

"Definitely," replied George. "

Mary used the device to scan the signal in George's metallic arm. The device showed green from his shoulder to his fingertips. She scanned his leg and halfway down the prosthetic, just above the knee, the signal turned from green to orange, then to red.

"Found something?" asked George.

"It's the femur relay," Mary said. "They can wear out after some time. I'll need to replace it."

"Appreciate it," said George. "I can't thank you enough for your help with all of this."

"Believe me, George," said Mary. "You already have."

The following morning, in lieu of breakfast, Mary, with Shandy riding shotgun, drove toward the exit of the base. Mary tried to be relaxed and discreet when the guard at the gate ordered her to stop her vehicle. Her anxiety rose slightly as the guard approached.

"Good morning, ma'am," said the guard. "Heading off base?"

"Just running an errand," said Mary.

"Please wait here for a moment," replied the guard.

Mary felt her heart rate increase as the guard entered the guard shack. He looked down at his desk, made a quick phone call, then peered through the window at Mary's vehicle. Mary rubbed Shandy's neck to try to help herself relax. The soldier went into the back room of the shack and solicited the help of another guard. The two exited the shack and approached her vehicle.

"Excuse me, miss, we need you to get out of the vehicle," ordered the guard.

"Is there a problem?" asked Mary.

"We need to search the vehicle," instructed the guard. "Please come with me."

The guard led Mary to a spot a few feet from the vehicle. She called Shandy out of the vehicle and had him sit next to her. Shandy barked at the guards as they went through the vehicle, so Mary knelt down and hugged the dog to quiet him. Because the car was a rental, it was very tidy, and the guards were able to check the car within minutes.

The first guard approached Mary and handed her a slip of paper.

"You are all set, ma'am," said the guard. "Apologies for any inconvenience. This is your pass to re-enter the base."

Without a word, Mary took the paper, smiled, and opened the car door for Shandy, then got into the driver's seat and slowly sped away. She patted his head as she headed into town, checking her rearview and side mirrors for any signs that she had been followed. She parked in front of a UPS store, looked around, and seeing no one she recognized, got out of the car and lowered the passenger window. She came around to the passenger side and, opening a small container hidden within Shandy's collar, took out several vials of medicine Mary had confiscated the night before. She opened the car door and raised the window.

"Stay here, boy," Mary said before closing the door. "I'll be right back."

Mary finished her three-week "tour of duty" as she liked to call it, and returned to Oklahoma, but instead of heading straight home, she was urged by her brother to meet him at her mother's house. They drove straight from the airport, forgoing food along the way to make the trip end that much quicker. Mary was apprehensive, her mind racing as she made her way along the roads to her mother's house. Bruce called several times, but Mary refused to answer. She did not want to get any bad news about her mother via a phone call and although this added to her anxiety, it made her focus on the goal of reaching her mother's house at all due speed.

She slid the car onto the grass in front of the house. She leaned over to the passenger door and flipped it open so Shandy could exit the vehicle. Together, they raced toward the house, noticing numerous cars parked in front of the residence. As they got close to the door, Mary could see Bruce's figure in the window, which suddenly made its way to the front door as she approached.

"How is she?" Mary asked as she barreled towards the door.

"You didn't pick up when I called," exclaimed Bruce.

"I was driving," Mary retorted. "How is she?"

"Go see for yourself," Bruce replied. As she passed her brother, Mary thought she saw the slightest hint of a smile.

Mary rushed into the house, passing an assemblage of relatives and friends. Food adorned the tables and glasses were scattered atop the furniture. Mary went straight to the den where she had last seen her mother.

Her mother sat in her chair, but the blanket she was wrapped in the previous time Mary visited was gone. And instead of distance, vacant eyes, Mary was greeted by the bright eyes and genuine smile of her mother. Her mother looked at her, a smile glistening her face.

"Mary?" said her mother. Her voice was soft, but clear. "Mary, how are you dear?"

"Mom?" Mary replied, her eyes welling with tears. "Oh, Mom, it's so good to see you."

"It's good to see you too, dear. I've missed you."

Her mom stood up from the chair and gave Mary a warm embrace. Mary hugged back, trying to be gentle but wanting to wrap her arms around her mother so tightly. She gently placed her head on her mother's shoulder. "I've missed you."

Mary pulled herself away and found her brother. Bruce wandered to a secluded section of the house so he could talk to his sister in private.

"You got the package?" Mary said.

"Of course I got it," replied Bruce. "What was it?"

"Medicine," replied Mary.

"Where did you get it?" asked Bruce.

"Let's just say a dark cloud brought it to me, Bruce," replied Mary. "That medicine was the sunshine I was looking for."

Leonard's World

by Michael Geisser

. . . N is for 'nothing.' It's the only word I know that follows 'noteworthy,' which was the word I used last time. I'm not sure whether 'nother' is a word so 'nothing' will do just fine. Nothing happened today, as every day for the past twenty-eight years. Things happened to others and in other places, but to me, here, nothing. I think you have to be a part of something, or else what happens, as far as you are concerned, is nothing. I remember when I was something and things happened to me, but not too clearly now. I've given up hoping for that place again. To be there again, I would have to be involved and that is not possible now. I might qualify as an expert on nothing; I've had so much of it. It's funny, but today I think my right pinky moved, not voluntarily, for I have no idea how to wish a movement into my body anymore, or at least I don't think it was voluntary. I don't even now know the feeling, if there is one, of having an active connection between my brain and my muscles.

What would qualify as silence for others is a festival of sound for me; I hear the air scratching against the walls, through the lattice on the headboard, across the floor, around corners and boxes and furniture. I hear insects on their flight paths and touching down, the drone of cars and trucks near and far, the patter of others around me, their breathing and clothes rubbing on their skins, my own assisted breathing. Some sounds I can't identify, even though they return, some regularly, some sporadically, so I give them names like steam train, cowbell, guitar string, fart. I wonder, not really wonder for I believe it won't happen, but I like to dream that I will someday put real names to these sounds, or know them personally, like a person who can investigate such things.

While I'm at it, and I've got the time, lots of it, my vision is still good, although I only get to use it at eight in the morning and eight at night. That's when a nurse, it could be any of a number of them, opens my eyes, one at a time, shines a light into them, shock and awe for me, releases them, makes a quick small notation on the chart and leaves. So, my visual experiences are fingers and hands, blinding light, the dirty ceiling with several cobwebs hanging down, and the occasional peripheral data if the nurse moves my head to get a good handle on my eyelid. I still remember colors, especially deep sky blue, like my eyes, as my favorite; it always drew me to the sky like a magnet. It's amazing how I can talk to myself. It boggles my mind that I don't think instead of talking as if there are two of us.

Since the accident . . . I was twelve years old and almost home when I heard it rattling right behind me, a rattle of great velocity, almost on top of me before I knew what to think. A car of some sort; that much I know. But I never saw or felt it. Well, I felt it for a second, the pain so great I melted into it so I wouldn't be its enemy, part of the pain, not the feeler of the pain, looking out from inside the pain instead of being its victim, like being the gun and not the target. Since then I've wanted to ride my bike again, free, wind-blown, speeding through the air like a rocket. Kids don't get much chance to be free; that was so special.

The first days were almost unbearable. I could hear everything my family and the medical staff said. They wanted me to "hang in there," to "fight, Leonard, fight!" Mostly it was my mom's voice that I heard, close to my ear, too close, too loud. I just wanted it to be over, to get back onto my bike, to eat my dinner in hopes of a good dessert, to have my dad carry me to bed. Well, he didn't really do that anymore then, but he did go with me and talk to me, instead of reading me a story, something that he'd stopped doing when he could no longer get through one without my questions interrupting him continuously. I wanted to scream after the first day, but nothing happened, almost like I was not there, looking out from a small TV camera implanted in my eyes, with me really being in the next room, or next state, or next country. That made it even worse, not being able to scream, trapped so deep that I became terrified of where I was, tied down, naked, buried alive.

After several months, I would have a day once in a while when I wasn't so terrified that I could almost think about what had happened and where I was, and what the future could be, hope perhaps. It was only after about five years that I finally made peace with myself, resigned that I may never get out, never eat a popsicle in the hot sun again, never just walk away from something, never fart and then laugh about it with friends, never . . . That was just the beginning, though, that was just the end of the descent. The real work since then has been to create a life anew from scratch, to move beyond the wreckage and scars from the terror and despair and build, atom by atom, a new reality, one that I could live within like a 'normal' human being, one that had room to move, at least psychologically. I think I'm almost there now, but it's never really done, is it? It's simple to get through a day now, in one sense. The secret desire to be like others, like I want to be, breaks above the waves sometimes, but it sinks away again as my thoughts wander to another island.

I'm sure people would be surprised if they knew what a vocabulary I have now. When I entered this monastery, I spoke and understood as a twelve-year-old, but listening to the talk around me hour after hour, day after day, month after month, year after year, eon after eon, I've learned millions of new words. Maybe not millions, but there are not many that I don't know when I hear them, and not many that I haven't incorporated into my speech, well, my speech to myself. I have even given shape and color to things that I've never seen, like a computer, that fits well into the conversation, although I'm sure that if I saw one, maybe felt it, smelled it, tasted it, although I don't think one would taste a computer, it would look different, maybe drastically so, from what I imagined. I could probably write a book about what I imagined and make a fortune by explaining things in such an alternative way that readers would pay money just to go to that world, my world.

I'm still wondering about that pinkie. Was it really a movement that I felt, or was it just a wish, or a dream, or a rogue nerve cell playing tricks on me? There *has* been a new, almost tingling throughout my body lately, most likely another cold or another infection from the bedsores, but still . . .

O is for 'ovoid.' I know it comes after 'opossum,' but there must be other words between. Regardless, I don't know of one right now. What a word, 'ovoid.' When would you use such a word? Maybe in poetry. *The ovoid echo of the shipwreck* . . . I guess poetry isn't my bag. What are the parts? Is it o-void or ov-oid? I think it's ov-oid, ov-like. What is an 'ov'? Oval? I'm sure there are persons who think like this all day, every day. How could they ever talk fast or think fast? They would be forever stopping to analyze every syllable, reveling in their complexity instead of surfing across the sea of language at the speed of wind. I'm shutting down now to the pace of a slug, just wandering about in my head, no plan, no effort, sleep.

Awake again, another day. Sleep, like what I just finished, is often just a nodding to a lower energy level, like when a computer is sleeping, I think. Often, like now, I'm put back into wake mode when the nurse shines that light into my eyes. Now *that's* a wake-up call. Oh, for the days when my Mickey Mouse alarm clock would bray and jingle me awake to slurp mom's fresh-squeezed orange juice, feel the comforting womb of the hot shower, see the sun-painted shapes on the floor across from my window.

My mother is coming. She's still at least five minutes away, but I hear her helloing at the front desk or some checkpoint. Her walk sounds tired, but she's carrying something. Something small, for her step is just a little heavier than her lightest. Her breathing, now presenting, is hollow and raspy like she's eaten fur. I've noticed that the last few visits, old age (She would be what, sixty-eight, sixty-nine, now?) is resident. She's worn out faster since Dad stopped coming. She never mentions him, but I know he's died; her voice has changed to more edgy, more empty.

She's in the room, the sounds are screaming, flashing. And the smells are all reset. No more dusty, chemical institutional wafts; they've all been blown away by her wind, a wind suffused with sweat, not athletic sweat but the sweat of effort to maintain, and woman scents, like lilac, talcum and potpourri, faint today. She must've been up and dressed for a while. I wonder what time it is. It's so rare that I hear the time spoken.

"Hello, Leonard. How are you today? I'm sorry I'm late. I had to go over to your aunt Christine's to drive her to the airport. She's going to Wisconsin today to see your cousin, Wesley, and his wife, Caroline's daughter, get married. I remember when Wesley was born; his red hair and puckered mouth made him look like a wrecked fire truck. Gladys says your vital signs are good and you look fine to me, so I guess everything's all right. Today . . . let me just get out of this coat . . . today I'm going to read to you from *Bartlett's Familiar Quotations*. Your father always liked, likes, the way the sayings are wrapped up into high thoughts in simple packages. Every once in a while, he would use, uses, one when we are out, and he sounds so smart."

Who cares about *Bartlett's Familiar Quotations*; they're just thoughts for those who can't have their own. But Mom loves me, or feels obligated to show she loves me, or some other reason that I can't or don't want to fathom. So, overall, it's good that she comes. If she didn't come, I wouldn't have much of any human contact, even one-way contact. The nurses all think I'm already dead, just a heart pumping to keep the flesh from rotting, just another task in their day. Apply ointment where rashes break out, bathe me where grunge builds up, keep my feedbag full, or at least don't let it empty, change my urine bottle. Check, check, check, he's done. Ready for another day of existence.

The corroding drone of my mother's voice is beginning to fade as she tires. I would love to jump up and hug her, tell her to throw the book out the window, have her take me to a bar where we could have champagne and catch up on everything, although I don't know what champagne tastes like, something to do with grapes, or what it would do to me, how drunk feels. To make her laugh, to feel her face, faces are always so much softer than they look. Let her know that I've heard every word she's spoken to me these last twenty-eight years. That I've grown, just inside, but grown nonetheless, that I can think and feel my heart beating, can wish and hope, and have high highs and low lows just like everyone else. But these are just wishes leading to another low low. I wish I could cry.

Just about the time she was finishing the thousandth 'famous' quotation from Lord Byron (I would rather hear those of someone more contemporary, but I would rather hear lots of things else when I'm hearing something. I'm not part of the selection committee.) I think my pinkie moved again. Is this something like the phantom limb thing? And it wasn't just my pinkie. I also felt a stirring in my left leg. Is this good or bad? No way to tell, just wait it out. I'm good at waiting.

After Mom left, I returned to my game, thinking about every word I know. Just free association, not definitions, but the whole world, abbreviated, around the word. I thought this up a while ago to put some order in my life, which had been messy and undisciplined to the point that I was dying inside of boredom and hate. The hate wasn't for what was, but for what isn't. When I was first brought in here after the accident that was my last adventure, when I finally woke up and heard the doctors talking about me, I was sure that I'd soon be on the street again, riding the storm. I wasn't prepared to never speak again, never move again, never see much again, never ride again, never this, never that. The nightmare of not being able to tell the doctors that I could hear them, knew the answers to their questions, had preferences, desires, faded into hate. But that faded too. A sort of Zen peace took over, blunted the fear of dying from some simple error by another, perhaps the nurse's failure to clear the mucous from my throat so I suffocate, even though she'd checked it off her list. The lack of control becomes a kind of refuge, a state all its own.

It was then, during my eighty-thousandth reverie on existence that my eye blinked. I'm sure of it. And my pinkie moved again, I could feel the coarse blanket under it for the first time. I always wondered what the bed looks like. Then terror overcame me like a tsunami. What if this hope that was sprouting like a mushroom in the shit of my life was *not* the start of some change toward getting out of here? If I hoped even a little, just a peek, and it's proven false, I'd want to die instead of starting over the process of reconciling myself to this life again. I can't even kill myself, the ultimate freedom.

P is for 'perspective'. . . Huh, did part of my larynx stir as if a voice is being reborn? There are too many things going on. I want this, whatever it is, to happen slower, much slower. I feel torn, like a concentration camp survivor who is seeing food, real food, for the first time in years, knowing that if he takes more than a morsel the shock could kill him. Perspective . . .

Lost Soul

by Emily Tallman

Hope is a lot like a seed. You can nourish it, plant it in fine soil, fertilize it with encouraging words and let positivity flow over it. Keep it in a warm sunbeam and never let dark thoughts fall upon it. But sometimes, that seed can be plucked right out of the earth, crunched on, digested and carried far away to be shat from a bird flying over a city to fall in freezing wind and smash upon the cement.

I think my seed is crushed on a roadway somewhere, constantly being run over and ground into the asphalt by cars, drowned in oil and choked on exhaust. I'd say I have no hope left but somehow I still find myself wishing for one good day. A day where nothing goes wrong. Where work doesn't suck, people aren't disappointing, and no one dies. Thirty-four years old and I have yet to have that perfect day. Hell, I'd settle for a content day. Just a single day where nothing bad happens. Just once.

That day was not today.

I'm lamenting on that fact when I find myself walking down an alleyway, dark as the inside of a chimney, and I notice someone is following me. Someone with uneven steps that stomped along and would speed up or slow down just as I did. When those steps caught up to me, the body responsible for them pushed me into the brick wall of the seedy bar just three blocks from my apartment. I was so close to my pajamas and my sister and the promise of chocolate ice cream and raw cookie dough, but here I am, trapped in a cage made of heavy arms and legs.

"Hey there, sexy. What's a girl like you doin' in a shithole like this? You should have someone protecting you from guys like me." He leaned in and crushed my lips against my teeth with his, forcing my mouth open and filling it with the taste of stale beer.

I spat when he pulled back and then I bore my eyes into his, making it clear that I wasn't amused but I wouldn't put up a fight either. That was only what he wanted.

"What's wrong, love? Too stupid to figure out what's gunna happen next?" He laughed and I had to turn my head to escape the foul puffs from his mouth.

"If you're here to kill me you'd be doing me a favor. Just be a peach and let my boss know I'm not going to get in that mandatory overtime this weekend."

He looked down at me in drunken confusion and I had to roll my eyes. My jokes never really did fly. He took out a knife and watched it shine before pushing the blade against the skin of my neck. I felt the serrated edge against my racing pulse and couldn't help the swallow that followed. "Yeah, my doctor says I've got about a year to live so I figure my life is pretty worthless." At his look of narrow-eyed outrage I had to add, "Oh, but if you want to do me that favor, my business card is in the front pocket of my purse. Ask for Sally." I smiled at him. Probably not the wisest thing to do to my murderer, but why should he have all the fun in *my* last moments on earth?

Besides, I had been on the verge of suicide for quite some time. I wasn't going to bow down to fate. If I was going to die, I wanted some say in the how and when parts of the process. The only thing that has kept me from pulling the trigger at this point is the fear of what comes after death, but that fear hasn't stopped me from risking my life daily. It's just chance that I hadn't actually died yet. He really would be doing me a favor if he put an end to things.

He leaned forward and bit my neck, holding me in place while his fat, clumsy hand tore at the buttons closing my pants. Instinct told me to jerk my knee up into his groin, but I stood there placidly as he opened his pants and ripped my shirt to grope my chest. My neck was throbbing where his teeth had been.

God, men really were dogs.

"Hey you! Freeze." Someone screamed from the other end of the alleyway. I sighed, whether from relief or frustration I wasn't completely sure. This wasn't a dignified way to die to be sure, but I was almost dead, why did someone have to play savior?

My murderer slammed my head into the brick wall behind us before taking off at an awkward run away from the man who was threatening to shoot. I slunk slowly to the ground. The hit on the back of my head wasn't enough to knock me out, but it did have me seeing stars.

A gun fired and my murderer fell, screaming too much for it to have been a lethal shot. Hmmm, a dog and a coward, maybe he wouldn't have killed me.

Feet were headed towards me at a near-sprint before the man slid to a stop in front of me and tilted my head up. I heard him mumble something before he asked quickly, "Are you all right? I mean, did he hurt you? Were you stabbed?"

"No, thanks to you I'm fine," I said, laying on the sarcasm a little thick.

He looked at me as if not knowing what to think. Then, he got up in one fluid movement and ran towards the man he shot, apparently in the leg, to drag him to a car waiting at the end of the alley, putting him in the trunk before jogging back towards me.

Odd.

When he reached me, he offered his hand to help me up and averted his eyes. He took off his jacket and wrapped its warmth around me, hiding my bare chest. I clutched the fabric in one hand and my open pants closed in the other.

In a quick movement I barely noticed, he swept me up into his arms and headed back for the car. "Put me down!" I yelled, flailing in his arms.

Surprisingly he did. "Right, sorry. I should have asked first, you probably don't want to be touched right now."

"No, it's not that. I am perfectly capable of walking on my own," I said over my shoulder as I walked the rest of the way to the car. I opened the unlocked passenger side door and plopped in, relaxing into the cool leather seat and trying my best to ignore the screams coming from the trunk.

He got in the driver's side. "I thought I would have to convince you to get in the car. This is interesting."

"Why?" I asked, not looking at him but listening intently. This guy had a voice that could seduce you with math equations. Somewhere in the back of my mind a little voice whispered *dangerous*. I snuffed it out.

"Usually, rape victims are hesitant with people. Not trusting. Afraid. You're fine. Are you in shock?"

"Being the one in shock, I wouldn't know, would I? And besides, I wasn't raped, I was attacked, assaulted maybe is the right word. Maybe I am in shock but what good would going psycho do?" I said as he pulled my hand into his lap and checked my pulse.

"God, your heart isn't even racing. You must have nerves of steel."

"Nope, just don't have that little switch in my head that tells me I should preserve my life." He mumbled something to himself that didn't sound incredibly flattering. "What did you just say?"

"Nothing. It's just, you're the first known survivor of this asshole and you're friggin' nuts. I can't even imagine how much help you're going to be."

"I'm not crazy. I just live in a constant state of shit and wouldn't be bothered if someone put an end to it."

"What's so bad about your life then, that it just doesn't matter?"

I was quiet. He had no right to know anything about me. We rode in silence all the way to an abandoned warehouse, that wasn't so abandoned. When the car came to a stop, three men went straight to it and my knight in dirty dress clothes got out to open the trunk. They hauled out my would-have-been murderer and one of the beefier guys knocked him out and dragged him inside. My door opened and I was met with another surprised face.

"She alive?"

"Yeah." My knight answered from somewhere outside the car. "I lost him for a bit after he left the party, but I caught up just in time. We're lucky he follows a pattern."

"She okay?"

"I'm sitting right here, why don't you ask me?"

He smiled and helped me out of the car. When fully standing, I realized how dizzy I had been and swayed into him. My knight caught me securely in his arms and held me to his chest.

"Whoa, are you sure you're all right?" I had some trouble lifting my head, just the slight movement making the world blur around me that much more. My eyes focused in on something just to the right of the back tire of the car.

A tiny bud blooming in the crack of the empty lot. No room to grow, no food to absorb, constantly being crushed under foot, and yet it lifts its head back into the sun and perseveres. When all else fails, what do we do? We hope.

"Damn tumor," I mumble, looking up to fully grasp what the man holding me was asking but I felt my spine go limp and met only darkness.

An Introduction

by Belle DeCosta

Hello, little one. I'm your mom's mom, your grandmother. A bit formal, I know, but I have no idea what you will choose to call me. I do know whatever you decide will sound like angels singing to me every time you utter it. You see, you are already a precious being to me, the center of my heart.

Your mom tells me you are only the size of a strawberry, tucked all cozy inside her womb, your first nursery. No matter, it's never too early to get to know each other.

I can't wait to hold my hand on your mom's belly so you can feel my energy and I can feel yours! I'll most likely drive her crazy doing it often in the next few months, but I'm sure it's something she'll suffer gladly to bring the miracle of you into the world.

Your presence has long been awaited, little one, and there are many loving arms anxious to cradle you, none more so than mine. I can't wait to snuggle into your softness and feel the gentleness and innocence of your soul. To taste your sweetness when I smother you in kisses and to feel reborn every time you smile.

Oh, there is so much I want to teach you! Things like how to blow bubbles in your chocolate milk through a straw. How to tap dance, hug a tree, and embrace yourself. And how to properly play in the warm rain, face to the sky and dancing in puddles. How to doggie paddle, play Go Fish, and who to trust.

I want to show you that life really is a bowl of cherries, even with the pits. Yes, there is also a bowl of pits. Fortunately, it's a much smaller bowl and full of valuable lessons.

I look forward to encouraging you to think outside the box, to use your wonderful gift called imagination. And then sharing all the incredible, delightful things you will bring to life within your mind!

I want to teach you, by example, that it's more than okay to cry but never to whine. To make sure you know whoever stares back at you from the mirror is someone to be proud of as long as they are kind. Oh, and that the purest hearts you will ever meet have four paws.

I want to show you how exhilarating it is to color outside the lines! To let your dreams and creativity run free and see where they lead, and that ice cream sundaes make a great dinner. All in moderation, of course.

Or not.

I can't wait to stand in the woods with you, eyes closed, so your other senses can better share the life happening all around you. You'll hear the squirrels chatter, the chipmunks scurry, and the different birds conversing in their song. Together we'll breathe in the smell of the earth, the fallen leaves, the moss, and pine. You'll taste the honeysuckle on the wind and feel the vibration of rustling leaves. I look forward to watching your reaction as you face the sun, and it sinks into your pores and warms you like it does the water lapping against the rocks. I promise you it will all happen!

I intend to read to you endlessly, anxiously awaiting the day you can read to me. We can make up stories, both together and for each other. We will sing at the top of our lungs, laugh ourselves silly, and jump on the bed. I'll draw you two stick people, one tall and one short, holding hands on cloud nine, like your mom's grandmother used to do for her. And you will turn my fridge into an art gallery with your magnificent drawings.

I will love you, unconditionally.

I will make sure you understand that anything that lives in your heart is real and true. And yes, that includes Santa Claus and unicorns. Because as long as it lives in your heart and you believe, there is hope.

And I now know with hope, little one, all things are possible.

I know this because there is you.

Doctor Hope

by Steven R. Porter

Dr. Guenther Werner stared at the ornate, antique, eighteenth-century grandfather clock with both anticipation and dread, waiting for the hands to meet at midnight. He was determined to not stir from his easy chair one second before. As he waited, he wrung his wrinkled hands in his lap, picked at his tattered cuticles, stroked his straggly white beard, and distracted himself by thinking about the hundreds of thousands – perhaps millions – of revolutions the hands must have made around the tarnished silver and gold clockface since it had been created. He knew he wouldn't be around to see many more of them.

Earlier in the day, Dr. Werner's personal physician confirmed what he already presumed. He only had a few weeks to live, at best. The aggressive cancer he had been fighting for years had spread into his lungs, and even though he was being treated by one of the top oncologists in the country, he knew there was nothing more anyone could do. Each mouthful of air he pulled into his chest felt more labored than the last, and each step he took more challenging. His doctor's only advice was to get as much rest as he could, drink plenty of fluids, get his affairs in order, and make peace with the world. He was told that his ultimate fate was now in the hands of God.

He told his doctor to go to hell. He knew the end was in sight. He didn't need a mere physician to tell him that.

For the past fifty years, Dr. Werner had served as a tenured professor of neuroscience and psychology at Munich University in Bavaria. His work on the nature of brain waves and sleep patterns was revered worldwide, and he believed he was on the brink of an extraordinary breakthrough in the understanding and treatment of insomnia. Under his care, his test patients not only reported dramatic improvements in their sleeping conditions, but as a curious side effect to his unorthodox medications, they reported strange and bizarre occurrences of acute lucid dreaming – the ability to control and actively participate in their own dreams. Under Dr. Werner's care, his patients told fascinating stories of how they could fight off attackers in nightmares with great physicality, play a Beethoven sonata without training, and conquer any number of paralyzing anxieties and lifelong phobias. The experiences, they said, felt more real than reality.

As he watched the minute hand make its slow final lap around that old clock, he understood that because of his death, his work could never be finished. All those years in his lab, all those tireless experiments, all those sacrifices – all poised to be lost. All for nothing. Or worse, his achievements and notes would sit in some dusty archive waiting to be claimed by another researcher to call their own.

But now, as he looked on, he saw that the old clock had completed its purpose.

Dr. Werner covered himself loosely with a drab, wrinkled overcoat and began the slow labored walk across campus from his office to the apartment of his most recent star student, Lazlo Alberti. The air was frigid, and the short puffs of breath that emerged from Werner's damaged lungs created small clouds that were reminiscent of the great iron pufferbellies that rolled into the train station in his childhood hometown.

"Please sir, do you have any sense of what time it is?" Lazlo complained as the door creaked open, amazed at the sight of a stern Dr. Werner panting and shivering in the unforgiving December air. The doctor spoke slowly, to mock him.

"I know exactly what time it is! Do I look like a damned fool to you? I am keenly aware of every second, and I don't have too many of them left. Now get yourself dressed and follow me to the lab."

Lazlo's back stiffened. "If it pleases you, sir, I must respectfully decline. I have a final exam tomorrow and a thirty-page research paper due Thursday. I really need to—"

"What you really need to do is fetch your coat and follow me. Now do as I say. I will explain when we get to the laboratory. I won't use up much of *your* precious… *time*."

Werner's reputation among the hard-working student body was well-known and undisputed. He was the worst of the worst. He was arrogant, violent, abusive, and downright mean. He thought nothing of overworking a student and sacrificing their education and future for the sake of his research. But if a student were to refuse a direct instruction, they knew he could crush their dreams and hopes before their careers had even started. Lazlo had no choice but to follow, with no course other than to hope for the best.

* * *

The sleep lab was a cavernous, sterile, windowless place with thick walls and searing fluorescent lights. A dozen identical empty steel cots were lined up against the pale cinderblock walls. The room was optimally designed to be dark, dull, and quiet to assist patients with their sleep, but it looked far more sinister, like something out of a 1950s horror movie. There were no patients currently undergoing treatment, no students were allowed access to the lab after eleven, and the building custodians all went home promptly at midnight. Werner and Lazlo knew the lab would be vacant until the administrative staff arrived at seven the next morning. That would be all the time Werner would need.

"What can I help you with, sir?" Lazlo asked as he flipped up the lab's light switch, bringing the room flickering to life. "This is most upsetting. You understand I don't have proper clearance to have access to this building at this hour."

"Stop whining. This is my lab regardless of what the university thinks. I built it with these two old cragged hands, and I'm giving you all the clearance you need. I only require you for fifteen minutes, and then you are free to scurry back to the safety of your nest."

Lazlo sighed, clenched his teeth, and frowned. He had worked tirelessly for Dr. Werner the entire semester and didn't feel the sarcasm or insults were necessary. But they were not unexpected.

"So, what is it you'll have me do exactly?"

With new-found energy, Dr. Werner zigzagged back and forth across the room, gathering supplies, vials, and other gadgets. He piled them haphazardly on a table adjacent to one of the beds then plopped himself into it. His heavy frame caused the bed to creak, grinding steel against steel, and Lazlo winced, expecting it to spring apart.

"You are going to help me go to sleep."

Lazlo froze as Dr. Werner assembled the equipment. The doctor was strange, but this was a level of bizarre beyond even his character.

"You want me to do what… exactly?" Lazlo sensed what was about to happen, and he wasn't too happy about it.

"You will initiate me into the sleep study protocol. Fetch that IV stand and roll it over here. Now!"

Dr. Werner's booming voice echoed throughout the empty hall, bounding from cinderblock wall to cinderblock wall, causing Lazlo to spring into action. Following Dr. Werner's lead, Lazlo secured him to the bed, then prepared the IV and stabbed a needle into one of the protruding blue veins on the doctor's right arm. Lazlo was trained to perform this routine on the sleep-study patients in Dr. Werner's control groups, but never considered he would be doing it to the doctor himself. After a few minutes of fiddling with the tubes and arranging the supplies, Lazlo stepped away.

"Is there anything else, sir? I really should go."

"Yes, there is one more thing."

Dr. Werner reached into his pocket and produced a glass vial of greenish-blue liquid that he slapped into the palm of Lazlo's hand. Lazlo twirled it in his fingers, then looked down at Dr. Werner.

"Is this the same solution you give to your insomnia patients?"

"That's none of your business. Just add the entire vial to the IV bag at once."

"The entire vial? But you've only ever prescribed a drop or two at most."

"Just do as I say and then leave the room."

Lazlo grimaced, then complied. Now alone, Dr. Werner fell asleep within minutes.

He soon began to dream.

* * *

It wasn't long before Dr. Werner realized he was immersed in a lucid dream. And he was fully cognizant of his surroundings. He found himself standing in the great room of an old hunting lodge, and around him were dozens of objects that at first sight had no connection to one another. There was a set of golf clubs, a simmering bowl of chili, a broken banjo, empty flowerpots, and so many other seemingly random items. He glanced around and took a quick inventory, recognizing each of the haphazardly arranged pieces from different dreams he had experienced through the years. Everything was recognized, yet none of it belonged together. It was much like walking through a garage sale from a lifetime of dreaming, or the prop room of some random second-rate Hollywood movie. He picked up a book from a nearby coffee table and cracked it open. Inside, he saw hundreds of words but was unable to read any of them. He thought for a moment about his favorite book, *Robinson Crusoe*, and in an instant the book transformed into a brand-new copy. He thought about how nice it would be to crawl into one of the easy chairs in the corner and spend a few hours of relaxation and reading.

But no. He was here for a different purpose.

Dr. Werner set the book down and opened the creaky wooden lodge door. Outside, the sky was bright and the air warm. It was a spectacular spring day – no painful December chill here. He glanced up at the peculiar turquoise-colored sky and noticed there was no sun to be seen. And then as if on cue, one appeared directly overhead but curiously, his oversized body cast no shadow. Without haste, he began to walk across the plush green lawn and spectacular flowered gardens toward a pond he could see a few hundred yards ahead.

He reached the grassy shore of the pond and seated himself near the edge. Noticing that his shoes and socks had disappeared, he dipped his feet into the cool water, wiggling his toes and breathing in the sweet fragrant country air. He felt no symptoms from his soon-to-be-fatal medical condition. He glanced at his watch to check the time, but realized he wasn't wearing one. Here, he surmised, conventional time did not matter anyway. A deep cleansing feeling of contentment washed over him.

"Guenther, do you know how long I've been waiting?"

A voice shot out from behind and pierced through his mind like an arrow. Dr. Werner sat up straight. Then spinning and stumbling, he bounced to his feet. As he looked down at his wrinkled clothes and protruding stomach, he felt embarrassed. He had not taken good care of himself, and here he was meeting Amelie for the first time in over fifty years, and she looked exactly as he remembered her. Her hair was golden and curled and seemed to dance on her shoulders even when she was still. Her eyes were round and blue, and her light summer dress fluttered with rhythmic grace in the affable spring breeze. She still looked to be twenty-two years young. She had not changed a bit.

"I wanted to come sooner. I really did," Dr. Werner pleaded. His stern demeanor was now gone, and the nervousness that wavered through his voice made speaking awkward. "I promised I would come to you again, and I kept that promise."

"So, is that why you are here? To fulfill a promise you made fifty years ago?" Amelie walked a small circle around him. "Is that why I've been waiting here all this time?"

"No. Of course not. I would have come sooner. I wanted to… desperately. But I couldn't. For the longest time I didn't know how. My research wasn't done. It would not have worked. I had to wait."

"So you've completed your research – your first love – and you've come to see me. Now. After all these years."

"Please understand. Every day of my life, I looked for you. When I first arrived at the university, each semester, when the new students arrived on campus filled with energy and enthusiasm, I would stare out my office window and look for you among the crowd. Every trip to the market, I would search up and down the aisles. Every stroll I took through town, I would peer into the shop windows. I was convinced you existed somewhere in my earthly world, in flesh and blood, and you were not just a delusion I imagined out of a single random dream from fifty years ago. I fell in love with you that night and I felt you were always nearby, always with me. I had to believe you were real."

"I fell in love with you, too. I never forgot you. You were always with me, too. It was a beautiful night. I've often wondered what it would have been like had you never left me. And by the way, I am real. And I waited."

"Of course, I believed you to be real. It was what drove me – it was that great hope. You were a reality that was more beautiful, more colorful, and more enticing than anything I could find in the world I live in. I tried to get back to you in my dreams when I went to bed each night, but when I woke each morning, I could remember nothing of you. My dreams were instead filled with random and inane images of silly, surreal things and unimportant places. This is what has fueled my university research programs all these years. I experimented on all those patients to break the lock and open the gates to my own dreams for no other reason than… to find... you."

Amelie wrapped her arms around his shoulders and laid her head on his chest. He was surprised to feel how delicate Amelie felt wrapped by his arms. She felt so warm and soft as he caressed her back. Dr. Werner closed his eyes to savor a moment he had longed for most of his life. When his eyes opened, he was astonished to find they were now standing together on the deck of a ship. The ocean was choppy, and waves battered the hull, sending fine mists of spray over their heads.

"What happened? Where are we?" Dr. Werner glanced around. The ship was not something he had recalled ever dreaming about before.

"We have found each other again, but now it's time for us to go." Amelie said. Dr. Werner felt different. His protruding belly was gone, replaced by the slim, angular look of his youth. The muscles on his forearms were strong and well-defined, and on his head there was a black tuft of hair fluttering in the ocean wind. Even his beard and wire-rimmed glasses had disappeared. To anyone who saw him, he appeared to be a healthy, vibrant twenty-five-year-old again.

"Where are we going? I need to know."

"Well, do you now? You'll see when we arrive."

Dr. Werner felt out of control. It was a foreign feeling and he didn't like it. This wasn't supposed to happen in a world designed to be under his absolute command. He concentrated hard on the pond, the lodge, and the green fields, hoping to be transported back. But nothing happened. He was unable to control or change anything about his current surroundings. He pushed Amelie away.

"I suppose," Amelie said with a wry smile, "it's about time I keep you waiting for a while."

"I don't understand. Why are you doing this? This isn't what I wanted."

"I know. It's not what either of us want. We wanted to be together decades ago. Imagine the lives we could have had! But, as you know, that didn't happen. And now here we are."

"I don't understand. I've never seen a craft like this before. How could I be dreaming about it?"

"Because it's my ship. Or I should be clear, it belonged to my husband. My late husband."

"Husband?" Dr. Werner was stunned and stepped backward. "How could you have had a husband? I didn't dream you to be married."

"I waited. Then I waited more. Then I got married. My husband, Andre, was a career Navy man. We met at a small café in Spain when he was on leave one weekend. I had never met anyone with such a crazy sense of humor. A day never went by that we didn't laugh together. We were married for thirty-four years, then quite unexpectedly, his heart gave way. You wouldn't expect such a happy, big-hearted guy like Andre to have a weak heart. I was devastated. But our children were amazing and helped me through it all, otherwise I don't think I would have made it."

"Children?"

"Yes, our son Martin didn't leave my side for days. I think you'd really like him. The two of you would have a lot in common. He graduated from medical school and now works at a hospital in New York City. We had a daughter, too - Sylvie. She lives with her husband in Florence, Italy, where they run a little family restaurant. She is a master chef. I adore going to visit them, as well as my grandchildren, every summer. I am so proud of them."

"But this is all preposterous! You are the construction of a dream. How could you have lived such a life?"

"But a moment ago, you acknowledged I was real. Did you expect someone as real as I am would just stand in place and wait for fifty years… just like you did? You will have to tell me sometime how you define 'real'?"

Dr. Werner's heart pounded and he shouted in desperation. "But Amelie, there is something I need to tell you — I'm dying. I don't have long."

Amelie paused, then gazed up into his panicked eyes.

"Yes, I know. That's why we are here together now, isn't it? We all die sometime."

Dr. Werner discovered he could no longer speak nor move. From the bow of the ship, he could see nothing but sea in every direction. And there was no horizon.

* * *

Lazlo had not been able to sleep. The more he stared at the ceiling, the more he came to realize the terrible mistake he had made leaving Dr. Werner alone. The man was elderly and not at all well, and was a tad crazy, too. Now Lazlo found himself standing in the lab at the foot of the bed staring at Dr. Werner's cold, stiff body, tubes still attached, wondering if he would be blamed for his death, or worse, arrested as an accomplice to his suicide. He feared for his reputation, education, and career, but felt nothing for the doctor. Emotionally, Lazlo felt no remorse, except the deep pangs of guilt that haunted him for despising this unfortunate excuse for a person.

He wondered if the doctor, who he believed had been tormented by some unknow demon his entire life, was now free of his suffering and in a better place. And he wondered if anyone would care.

* * *

In their parents' bedroom of their childhood home, Martin and Sylvie Moreau sat vigil next to Amelie's bed as she slowly succumbed to her illness. She had been sick for months, and was sent home by the hospital days before to more comfortable surroundings when it was deemed there was no more they could do for her. And now, over the course of the last few hours, her condition had worsened, and she had become unresponsive. Under Martin's loving medical care, and with great anguish, they watched as little by little, the last bit of what had been a happy, robust life drifted away.

"Do you think she still knows we are here?" Sylvie asked her brother through gentle tears as she held her mother's frail hand.

"Yes, I do. If nothing else, I believe she can at least sense our presence."

"She was talking in her sleep again last night," Sylvie said, a bit concerned. "But I could tell she was not speaking to me. At first, I assumed she might be imagining that she was talking to Daddy, but I had the distinct impression she was communicating with someone else. She kept repeating, *I waited, I waited.* I can't imagine what that could mean."

"I wouldn't spend too much time analyzing it," Martin said as he sat on the corner of the mattress, posing like some TV soap opera doctor, which he knew would have made their mother laugh. "My guess is that it was just a garden variety dream. I don't know if you know this, but there's a fine line between the dream state and clinical delirium as the waves that manage both originate essentially in the same region of the brain. It's the brain's way of repairing itself, resolving unresolved conflict, I believe — solving problems. It's Mother Nature's way of helping one of its grand, fading creatures find its peace. Or then again, some would speculate that it's just a few random synapse connections firing off."

"I've always thought dreaming to be special. Like a gateway to other worlds, hopes, and aspirations. Life is so limiting, and so predictable at times. Why should we restrict ourselves to one life? I like to think dreams can always come true. And you make it sound so dry and clinical."

"I'm sorry. It goes with the territory. I've been reading these Bavarian sleep study medical research papers on brain waves and dreaming. It is painfully dull stuff, I must say. But it has given me a few ideas. I'm thinking of expanding on this research in our new sleep study program at the hospital."

At that moment, Martin and Sylvie fell silent. Amelie had gasped and shuddered, then opened her eyes for the first time that day. Her once pretty blue eyes were now as dark as the sea. Amelie's eyes glanced past the faces of her adoring children and focused on the ornate, antique, eighteenth-century grandfather clock that stood in the corner.

The tarnished silver and gold clockface hands moved ahead one more minute. It was now five past midnight.

A Bluebird Sings

by Jess M. Collette

Her days are long. Turning the clocks ahead for Daylight Savings Time hasn't helped. Daylight has encroached on the night and this change has tested her sanity. She listens to the ticking clock. Its hands are not only playing with time but they're also toying with her, piercing through her. The shine of their brass is blinding. After surviving another cold, dark winter she wanted to feel better with the arrival of spring, but not even the appearance of the first blossoms, white and purple crocuses breaking through the frost-heaved ground, could shake the gloom. When the late-season snowstorm dropped a heavy blanket of white on April's flowers, bending them to the ground, she also felt defeated. In her bed, she hides beneath a heavy blanket of slightly darkened, once-white sheep's wool. It still has his scent.

His days are long. He heard the foreman say it was Daylight Savings Time, but he's forgotten what that means. His days have only grown longer and darker. Inside the mine, the day does not know night and night does not know the day. They are one and the same, yet he feels like he knows neither. He only knows the mine: the dark, the damp, the dreariness. His life is a tunnel with no end in sight. Though his timepiece ticks non-stop in his pocket, its mechanical clicks have long ago been lost to the background clatter of the mine. The clang of metal picks against rock constantly competes with the ramblings in his mind. He drives his pick into the mine's solid wall a little harder, begging for silence. A chunk breaks free and lands hard on his foot. He doesn't notice. He wipes the sweat from his brow with his tattered, coal-dusted shirt sleeve, soaking up the salty drops just before they flood his eyes. He still feels the burn. From his pocket, he pulls out a folded handkerchief, but it's not meant to clean his soot-smudged face. His fingers follow the lace-trimmed edges to the middle of the square. He traces the 'M' embroidered in its fabric even though the darkness hides its existence from his eyes. It's perfumed with her.

Her days are long. More flowers have appeared: yellow, blue, and red petals now speckle life on the drab brown of the earth. She has pulled back the curtains in every window, cleaned the glass panes to rid them of the dullness deposited by darker days, and hung the laundry on the line. She sits and rocks a bit on the front porch in the rocker he built. The air is clean, but the coolness remains. The weathered sheep's wool blanket keeps her warm. A chill runs down her back as she wraps it tighter around her shivering shoulders. His scent: cedar, bergamot, and a hint of whiskey, hugs her. The ghost of his arms holds her. Her eyes close. She's lost to the last amber-colored hours of daylight.

His days are long. Fresh off the train from Montgomery, more men arrive to work the mine. He wonders when he'll be allowed to board that same train back. At the entrance to the mine, he stops to get a glimpse of them. It's a much-needed distraction as he waits to hear the commanding voice of the foreman, the man who holds his and the other men's fates on his breath. The new arrivals are mostly young, with clean-shaven faces still shiny like the promise of morning. Their smiles of naivety are wide and white, yet to be narrowed and dulled by the gloom of coal dust. Today, there are some second-timers arriving with them: the haggard, unshaven, weathered souls with dead eyes. He knows them well. He fears he is one. The foreman doesn't offer a reprieve to any men today before he orders them to make their daily descent into the mines. He averts his eyes from the retreating foreman. He is numb. The weight of disappointment is crushing as he reaches inside his shirt pocket. A corner of the pocket is loose and folded over. Torn thread spins in the wind. He cradles a small picture in his bruised and calloused hands. The portrait is aged and faded. It has her eyes.

Her days are long. Morning welcomes the sun into the opalescent sky readying to turn blue. She tosses in bed to shake the sleep from her limbs. Stillness. The cabin creaks somewhere in another room as the old pine logs expand and contract with the changing day. Each day is different, each day is the same. She dresses in layers, remembering the heat of noon and the chilly bite from the end of yesterday. Her favorite sweater has softened over the years, the once stiff yarn has transitioned to balled-up fluff. She puts her arms through each sleeve and wonders how the sweater has avoided getting holes from the moths. Down the sweater's bumpy exterior, her hand dips into the oversized pocket. Old paper crinkles against her skin. Does she dare look at it today? The ragged edges of the ink-soaked page, folded in fours, tickles and tempts her hand. She sits at the kitchen table, steadying herself against the hand-hewn logs of the bench he made. A deep breath expands her lungs as she raises the paper from the sweater's hiding place. Opening fold upon fold, her eyes see the words he wrote. The paper is stained from the tears she's cried. She bites her lip as a witness to the imperfect mix of their emotions on the page.

My sweet Mary,
When the east winds blow the grasslands to the ground, know the time we've lost, soon will be found. The time draws near when the days are long, soon I'll be back with you where I belong. When the bluebird sings and makes its nest, with you my love I'll soon find rest.

Forever yours,
Luke

Exhausted from the day, she lies down in bed, hugging the tattered sheep's wool blanket. She's still wearing her favorite sweater. His note, their note, crinkles as she rolls to her side. Her eyes, heavy with the tears she refused to let fall earlier in the day, flood the pillow. She is empty. Sleep falls on her fast and heavy. She dreams of him.

His days are long. A couple of the new guys won't shut up. He's heard their names, the towns they're from and despite their constant prodding, he hasn't responded with any information about himself. Still, they keep asking. He doesn't remember one detail about any of them. They too have become nothing more than noise. Their stories are lost to the depths of the mine. He hits the rock and wipes his sweat repeatedly in the darkness. Hours go by, voices fade, tones deepen, laughter ceases.

In the stillness he finds rest. Her sweet laughter is in his ear, mixed with the words he wrote to her.

My sweet Mary,
When the east winds blow the grasslands to the ground, know the time we've lost, soon will be found. The time draws near when the days are long, soon I'll be back with you where I belong. When the bluebird sings and makes its nest, with you my love I'll soon find rest.

Forever yours,
Luke

With just enough strength left at the end of the day, he crawls into his cot. He doesn't even have the will to wash the grime of the mine away. The lumpy fabric of the mattress digs into his knotted back. He doesn't move. The pain will dull with time. He picks up the piece of cedar he brought from home and pops open his pocketknife. An unpolished but still sharpened steel blade springs forth. He still hears the promise he wrote for her as he whittles. Despite exhaustion, he works. With each feather carved into the aromatic wood, the likeness of a bluebird appears. It's his promise to return to her.

Her days are long. She watches the songbirds fly from the meadow, carrying the tall grasses in their beaks. They struggle to twist the unruly pieces into nests. She wants to help them, but she knows it's their struggle to overcome. They will be stronger for it. Two springs have passed and still, he has not returned. Will this be the year they both find rest? Her eyes drift to the empty hole in the cedar house that he made. She sweeps the last remaining debris of winter from the front porch. A dust cloud gathers and spirals up before being carried away by the gentle breeze. She watches it dissipate at the edge of the meadow where the tall cedars grow. A bluebird sings.

His days are long. More new men arrive. They already look tired. Their heads hang low from the oversized packs laying heavy on their backs. Their feet are dragging, kicking up dust on the dirt paths that snake down the hillside from the train depot to the basecamp at the mine.

He thinks about helping the new guys with the weight they carry. He knows it will only get heavier. It is their struggle to learn. They will be stronger for it. Two springs have passed since he first entered the mine, yet still, he has not returned to her. Will this be their year? His fingers run over the smoothly carved feathers of the cedar bluebird he carries in his torn pocket. The foreman calls his name. Time stands still. The tick of his pocket watch returns to his ears as he rides the moving steel of the locomotive toward home. As the train pulls into Montgomery, his hand grips her handkerchief tighter than he ever has before. He follows the path that's worn and familiar through the forest he knows. Remnants of coal dust drift from his clothes with each step. A soot cloud rises and is carried away on the gentle breeze. At the edge of the meadow where the tall cedars grow, he steps into the sunlight. A bluebird sings.

Married in Moscow

by Joann Mead

It was the Fall of 1980 in Moscow, Russia, back in the USSR. It was a year of change in my life and in the world around me. For me, it was a time of trepidation and excitement. For others, it was a time of disappointment. It was the year of dashed Olympian dreams for US athletes. The Soviet Union invaded Afghanistan and, in retaliation, the US boycotted the Moscow Winter Olympics.

So, instead of a summer job with NBC, ferrying film crews around to sports events, I traveled around the world with an Englishman. It was the beginning of something small and big and new for both of us.

When I first met Jim, we were the only two people who showed up for a US embassy tour of the Moscow Metro. An embassy staffer took us on an underground tour of the palatial stations where she pointed out the ornate frescoes, marbles, and chandeliers. Those grand ballrooms hidden below contrasted wildly with the stark, monolithic structures above on street level. But it was those huge "wedding cake" buildings above ground that prophesied our future.

As I walked by Jim's side, his arm brushed lightly against mine. Like electricity, the shock from his skin made my hair stand up on end. I felt a distinct tingling, but make no mistake, it was not one of those tingling feelings like "falling in love." He was, like me, another teacher, someone I'd be working with at the Anglo-American School. And, as a rule, I would never date another teacher. Oh no.

Jim said, self-mocking, that his sweat made his watch run backwards. "It's got something to do with the salt content of my skin."

I couldn't help but think that this guy was a bit weird. A pleasant, kind-of-cute, long-haired nerd—what the British would call a "boffin."

I wondered why this boffin would admit to an anomalous quirk of body chemistry that could reverse the trend of time. No, he was not my type. I still hadn't figured out what that type was, if there even was such a thing.

And then there was the night eight of us teachers piled into a van for an evening of skating on the flooded walkways of Gorky Park. On most winter nights, the flooded, frozen trails were well-lit. But as it happened, it was the coldest night of the year and all lights in the sprawling park had been turned off. The winding pathways were shrouded in eerie darkness.

The young and fearless of us coursed off in different directions. I paired up with two other women. Together we negotiated our way through an unfamiliar maze, snaking through the icy blackness of night. Gliding on blades along unfamiliar paths in this foreign, forbidden land was exhilarating.

An hour or more had gone by when we came across what looked like a statue. On closer inspection we found a guy, nearly frozen, anchored in a snowy side-bank. Trying to free his buried skates, he trudged laboriously, struggling towards us, slogging and clomping his way out of the frozen snow. It was Jim, shivering from the cold. He'd attempted a sport he had never tried in new hockey skates he had never worn before. We flanked him, propped him up, and found our way to an Olympic-sized ice rink where we met up with the others.

Jim, notorious as the mad Englishman, learned a lot of new things in Moscow, often by default. Not just how to ice skate, which he later mastered, but also how to drive a car. Most of us learned to drive in traditional ways with learner permits and lessons back in our home countries. But Jim? No. He never did things in conventional ways.

When it came to life's necessities, our respective embassies usually helped us. Apartments, cars, and the required Russian driver's license. I handed over my California license, which sufficed, and was issued a Soviet license I've kept until this day. I picked out my new car, a Lada Zhiguli, a ubiquitous boxy sedan, having walked around a big auto lot in Moscow trying to find a car that would actually start up. So many didn't—there were plenty of defectives.

Jim bought a second-hand Zhiguli from British diplomats. But the real hitch was, he didn't know how to drive a car. Unlike a new pair of skates, driving a car might be more of a challenge—the snow bank you end up in might lead you into the Volga River or skating across thin ice. But, you might ask, how did Jim procure a Russian driver's license if he'd never driven a car? He did have a motorcycle permit that the British Embassy turned over to the Soviet bureaucrats who, having not correctly translated it, issued a Russian automobile license to the mad Englishman.

Now, it's hard enough to find your way around Moscow using the inaccurate maps printed in Cyrillic that looks like an upside-down alphabet. I forever got lost, often for hours circling the perimeter of Moscow's inner ring road or hanging left turn *raznavorts*, a system of U-turns to reverse directions. There was no such thing as a simple left turn. Really. But Jim had to learn, not only how to handle a car's gear shift and how to brake while sliding on ice and snow, he had to figure out where he was in a language he didn't know and decipher an alphabet he couldn't read. Fearless, he persisted nevertheless.

No. It was not love at first sight. Funny how first impressions can be. Little did I know that Jim would become my best friend, in the *world*. It was the beginning of a new episode for both of us.

That summer was full of adventures that warrant stories of their own. From the scary, silent Russian authorities in the port city of Nakhodka—they tried to stop me (but not Jim) from boarding the Far East Steamship to Yokohama Bay—to the extreme turbulence while passing through the Sea of Japan where no one on board the steamship could eat, let alone hold down the squid meal Jim described as "high-grade rubber bands."

It was in Kyoto, Japan, at a restaurant on the Kamogawa River (Jim called it a sewer), where we dined on a wooden terrace, sitting on floor mats under a low table, eating tempura and drinking Kirin beer, that Jim asked me if I would marry him. Surprised by the unexpected question, I thought to myself that if I said yes, I could somehow get out of it later. I'd never said yes to anyone, although others had asked, but I always thought of proposals as some form of entrapment. I was pretty good at getting out of commitments of any kind. So, I crossed my fingers behind my back and said yes.

In the fall, after our journey on a one-way ticket around the world on the now defunct Pan Am airlines, a small thing happened.

I was cooking when Jim arrived at my apartment; he followed me to the kitchen. I'd visited the embassy doctor that day for what I thought was a minor problem. But he wanted to do a test. My diagnosis came back quickly and I was rewarded with a bottle of pills. I pointed to the pills on the kitchen countertop.

"Is this what he prescribed?" Jim asked, without reading the label. "Do you have something?"

"Yeah, I guess you'd say that I do have something." I couldn't resist a smirk. "Look at this, read it." I pointed to the label on the super-charged multivitamins.

Jim looked confused. It took a while for him to question the significance. "So, what are these for?"

"I'm pregnant," I said, matter-of-fact and looked up to see his reaction. "Those are prenatal vitamins."

He gasped, he squealed, he cried as he hugged me. It was a cross between happiness and hysteria. I was still in shock over the diagnosis. And pregnant in Moscow as a foreign quasi-diplomat would have its conundrums. Mostly, at this point, unforeseen.

Neither of us thought it an ill-fated pregnancy. It was something we not only accepted, but really wanted. We never mentioned our mutual trepidation about the little something that would change both our lives. Nor did it matter that we were living in a country that belonged to neither of us. It just added to the intrigue.

But now a new problem arose. How to get married in a foreign country, Russia, despite its diplomatic unease with both the United States and Great Britain. The British and American embassies gave us varied advice on our little dilemma. But we had hopes that we could fumble our way to a doable marriage.

But first things first. The embassy doctor's first concern was my IUD contraceptive device. Obviously, it didn't do what it was supposed to do. I could have it removed at a clinic in Finland but there were risks involved. The risk, about a 50-50 chance that the baby would not survive. There are no guarantees in life. So, we took the chance and hoped for the best.

We ventured on a journey aboard the Red Star express, the overnight train from Moscow to Helsinki. In a sleeper car for four, we took one side, me in the bottom bunk, Jim on top. Later, we were joined by two burly men who were travelling to the Arctic circle to work in oil and gas. They offered us vodka (typical of Russians) but we declined. It was a long night, but surprisingly, they were well-behaved.

At the clinic, the Finnish doctor asked, "Do you want this baby or not? It's your choice."

As I nodded a wide-eyed yes, he chuckled at my enthusiasm. "But you must stay for three days in Helsinki, just in case there are complications."

All went as well as we hoped for. On day three, we decided we would get married. But nothing is ever as easy as it seems. The easy part was buying a wedding band. I still wear it today, simple gold with a bamboo style. We easily found the courthouse where we could find out how to get married in Finland.

Jim asked a secretary our pressing question, showed our passports, and said we worked in Moscow at the diplomatic embassy school. She made a quick phone call.

"Oh, he isn't busy, you can see him."

Not quite knowing who "he" was, she escorted us to the most ornate office I'd ever stepped foot in. It was the chandelier, hand-carved Victorian sofa, an elegant conference table, and wooden cabinets full of beautifully embossed law books that spoke to the eminence of the office inhabitant, the Supreme Court Justice.

After introductions, feeling out of place in our blue jeans and jackets, we asked if we could get married in Finland as soon as possible.

"In Finland, a man does not need to be a resident, you could get married today. But a woman," the kind and friendly judge said as he looked at me, "you will need to be a resident for three weeks."

So, that put an end to the conversation, the dilemma, we didn't have three weeks of leisure to spare.

Back in Moscow, we made another visit to the British embassy. No, they didn't have the authority to perform marriages, but perhaps the British embassy in Kabul, Afghanistan might be able to help us? Or maybe the embassy in Spain? This was all getting a bit confusing and complicated. There had to be an easier way.

An American preacher lived downstairs from me. We asked him our question while waiting for our "steak-cheese-onion," a famous dish served up at the American embassy cafeteria. But no, he had no authority in Moscow to marry us, and in his opinion, he wouldn't marry us if he could because he "didn't think we were suited for each other."

Jim whispered, "Pompous ass."

In Moscow, we had another option. We could get married with a civil ceremony in a "Wedding Palace," usually in a baroque residence. In the Soviet Union, only ceremonies performed in a registry office or Wedding Palace could be "blessed" by the Communist Party. But with a five-month waiting time, I'd be looking like a party balloon ready to pop.

Jim told friends, a British correspondent and his Jordanian wife, about our dilemma. They had a friend who was the Orthodox emissary of the Antioch Church. At the time, under the separation of church and state, religious wedding ceremonies were not legally valid. But their friend, the orthodox priest, told them his church had been granted diplomatic status as a holdover from czarist times.

The priest usually conducted services in Russian, Arabic, and Greek but he also spoke French and English. He had an English translation of the official Orthodox wedding ceremony, printed in America, but he had never used it. But he'd be happy to try it out.

So here we were on a Friday, set up to get married on Sunday in the Antioch Orthodox church in Moscow. With neither of us particularly religious—me, a lapsed Roman Catholic from Los Angeles, and Jim, a lapsed Anglican from London—neither of us felt conflicted. All preparations were a whirlwind of ad hoc efforts by friends, from flowers to food to finding the way to the church. Their spontaneity and generosity meant there was little Jim and I actually had to do, it all just seemed to happen without us. We were merely actors in this short story of a most unusual wedding.

The small orthodox church, adorned with old icons, was now filled with an entourage of friends from the British, American, Canadian, and Australian embassies. The Lebanese priest, draped in a satin brocade robe of emerald green and gold, was flanked by Russian deacons and servers. Our Jordanian friend lent me her wedding gown, a white velvet kaftan. Her English husband was best man. Our bridesmaid, a Scottish friend. Both held very long tapered ceremonial candles that lit up the ceremony. Curious Russian women wandered in from off the street to see what was going on. A Bulgarian cameraman, married to a Canadian, took kilometers of film.

The dignified and scholarly priest shifted easily between English, Russian, and Arabic as he directed everyone on what to do. The orthodox ceremony and rituals were universal in message. The three sips of wine from the shared cup—the mutual exchange beckoned the doubling of joy, the dividing of sorrow. The sharing of hopes. The sharing of dreams.

The priest whispered as he placed two brass and velvet crowns on our heads, "Be careful, they are very heavy."

I wondered if the weight of the crown somehow signified the gravity of the vows. But then the priest swapped the crowns three times, back and forth between Jim's head and mine. I was struck with fear as we proceeded around the altar table, afraid my crown would fall off or my white lace scarf would alight from the burning flame of my bridesmaid candle. But we made it through the ceremonial first steps of our married life.

There was snow on the ground as we left the church and transitioned to more secular rituals. Following Russian tradition, a baby doll was tied to the front of the car—dressed in pink, it accurately prophesied the baby girl to come. On the balustrade of Lenin Hills were more wedding photographs overlooking the city of Moscow, followed by a warm reception and copious toasts of champagne with our friends.

A beautifully written, stamped marriage certificate signed by the Antioch Dean in Moscow and the Lebanese Ambassador immortalized our marriage ceremony. But the question now was, were we legally married in the eyes of the Soviet Union? For church weddings to be legal, they must be registered in the country where they are performed. So, should we try to register ours with the Soviet civil authorities?

Six weeks later, it was Christmas. We flew to Los Angeles. The next morning, we piled into two cars with my family and arrived late night in Las Vegas.

"Should we eat breakfast first or get married?" we asked when we gathered the next morning.

Everyone agreed. "Get married."

A quick visit to the justice of the peace, who stood at a counter wearing a string tie, was all we needed, unlike today where wedding chapels and Elvis themes are the norm. Our marriage certificate, recorded in Clark County, Nevada, is the legal one. It states our domicile as Moscow, Soviet Union.

1980. It was a year of the unforeseen, the unusual, the unplanned. A year of happenstance, accidents, chance coincidences and serendipity. Decisions weren't contemplated, we just made it up as we went along. And hoped for the best.

Sands in Time

by Alexander Smith

"Mango. Mango con chili."

The fruit vendor's smile shone like a second sun, and the warm, salty breeze swam on the beach. He wore a floppy hat and carried a cooler, peddling freshly cut fruit in plastic bags.

Through casual banter with his customers, the vendor seemed to know the smallest details about their lives, even ones they could not remember sharing. I know because I asked them about it and from my own experience, of course. Each time I heard his call that summer, I put down my book about Incan history and bought some fresh fruit.

He was an enigma. A mystery. Better than fiction. And I loved it.

One late August afternoon, when I was about to leave my post on the sand, I heard his call. I bought a bag of mango and patted him on the shoulder saying, "See you tomorrow, friend."

His smile beamed. He said, "No. No. No, you won't, *mijo*."

"No?" I said. "Why's that?"

But he had already left me behind. He walked down the beach. I couldn't see his smile, but I heard his call. "Mango. Mango con chili."

I left for my aunt's house and wondered what the fruit vendor meant while I weaved through the people on the boardwalk. All summer he had been selling fruit on the beach. Why wouldn't he be there tomorrow?

I refused to miss a single day outside during my summer stay in Venice, California. The weather was perfect. And being so close to the beach, I would have regretted missing an hour, let alone a day, of sun. So, every morning, I walked to the sandy edge of California with a book and a beach towel. The beach was an oasis from the chaos of Venice, with its self-proclaimed wino singing for drinking money, tattoo parlors outnumbered only by smoke shops, and tourists, lots of tourists. The sand a few dozen yards beyond the boardwalk was an oft-ignored oasis. Because of Venice's rough history, most people didn't trust the sand and water. But I saw no sign of used needles during my summer there, no matter how many people warned me away.

Venice was a curious place, and the fruit vendor's prophetic remark only added to the town's inscrutability.

I wanted to become an archaeologist. So, I put my hopes in the year-long fellowship that I applied for before my college graduation. But I only made the waiting list. I was disappointed. No one was going to drop such a prestigious international program. Plus, my pragmatic half knew that if I heard nothing by late July, it wouldn't happen. I wouldn't go to Peru and that made me sad. To cheer me up, my aunt invited me to spend the summer at her two-bedroom place in Venice. It was a good consolation prize. The time on the sand had given me so much. Best of all, a chance to loosen the reins on my future and allow things to happen.

Back inside, I threw my beach shorts and towel into the hamper and put on comfortable sweats cut off at the knees. I booted up my laptop to learn more about the digs happening around Cusco. Out of habit, I checked my email first. Among the junk was one marked 'URGENT.' And it came from the archeological fellowship.

Due to a cancellation, today, the email read, a slot had opened.

I called their office immediately.

"Excellent," the fellowship administrator said, "we're excited to have you on board. We're so sorry everything is so abrupt. Orientation begins in Peru on Monday, so we need you there as soon as possible. Your flight leaves LAX tomorrow morning. When you land in Lima, the program's shuttle will come to the airport to pick you up."

"I can't believe this!" I said. Despite my attempt to maintain a professional facade, I couldn't hide my childish excitement.

"Check your email for the details. Just print them and get packed. I can tell you're eager to work with your peer team on this Incan excavation."

I buzzed the rest of the night.

* * *

By November, I had no doubt that I'd been paired up with the love of my life.

I now stood behind her as she knelt in the dirt, peering at the cracked ceramic jar she had just exposed. She reached her hand back, and I knew, without her saying, that she needed the dusting brush.

A recent Harvard graduate, Ladhi had been born on the coast of western India, in a small village south of Mumbai. Her two parents, both prolific lawyers, had relocated to London when she was young.

I first met her while switching planes in Panama. She wore tan khaki shorts and hiking boots and looked like she belonged at a dig site. Compelled by something beyond me, I approached her.

"You look like an archaeologist," I said.

"You're very perceptive," she said. "I'm actually flying to Lima. I'm part of an archaeology fellowship."

She extended her slender, unadorned hand to me. I was speechless for a moment. Then I managed to give her my name. We talked, and I learned that she was also part of my program. When it was time to board, we took adjacent seats on the plane. Spurred on by complimentary airline drinks, we chatted all the way to Lima.

During the second half of the fellowship that spring, we were inseparable. Although a world traveler, Ladhi had yet to see Los Angeles, and through email, my aunt urged us to visit Venice after our program concluded. We agreed and planned the arrangements.

In June, before the dig-site fellows prepared to leave, we all exchanged hugs and contact information. I had made many friends I'd remain in contact with for years. But Ladhi was different. I didn't want to spend any more of my days apart from her.

At Jorge Chávez International Airport, Ladhi and I sat in reverent silence while we sat on the old seats waiting to board. We didn't need to speak. We were both still soaking in the wonderful experience.

* * *

The Los Angeles sun woke me from a dreamy reverie. I rolled across the beach towel onto my side.

My arm touched Ladhi's warm skin and stirred her from shallow sleep. I pulled closer to kiss her full, dry lips.

My aunt had picked us up from LAX and offered us an avocado-accented dinner. We had sat at her small table overlooking the canals. Today our plan was to lounge on Venice Beach and tour Hollywood that night. Ladhi had never been to LA after all.

Then, I recognized the call.

"Mango. Mango con chili."

I jolted up and saw the silhouette of my fruit vendor. I waved him over with both hands.

"*Mijo*," he said, "Welcome back. Did you meet the Incas like in those books you always read?"

"Yeah, but wait," I answered in disbelief. "Who told you I was in Peru?"

"News travels," he said. "Like you."

He handed Ladhi and me each a bag of spiced mango. He waved away the folded dollars I offered.

"Last August, you said you wouldn't see me," I said. "How'd you know I'd get the fellowship and leave the next day?"

"Ah," he said with a sparkle in his eye. "That's a secret, my friend."

His smile outshone the sun. He turned to go, but I still felt his radiance.

Before he could disappear, I had to know. "My friend, will I see you tomorrow?"

"Yes! See you tomorrow, friend."

I smiled and held Ladhi next to me. She opened her bag of fruit and picked out the largest piece.

The fruit vendor continued north along the beach. The sun and the sand together consumed his form. It was only an illusion, I knew, but he appeared gone, disappeared into the vastness of it all. Only his call yet echoed in the sands of time. "Mango. Mango con chili."

Beneath the Cove

by Pete A. O'Donnell

School was out, but the summer was off to a slow start. Underneath gray skies and drizzle the cove was slightly warmer than the bottom of an iceberg. Last week it'd been close to 90 degrees, teasing Mason while he took his final exams. Now, his first day off, the day he was going find it, the thermostat nosedived. He stood at the water's edge, taking off his t-shirt, shivering as he stepped in.

No one was around. Mason felt ridiculous with his father's mask on, reacting like every other human who'd ever made the choice to step into cold water. He clenched up, twisting his face and biting his lip, making a pitiful sound as the water reached his waist.

And why was Mason doing this? He was looking for something, but he wasn't certain what it was. There was a mystery beneath the cove, something he'd touched on a cold winter's day.

He glanced at the woods, remembering the cove covered in ice. It leaves an impression when you almost die, especially in a very stupid way. If you have to die, you should try never to leave anyone saying, "Well, that was dumb." Take that as a warning and don't ignore it like Mason ignored the warning from his father.

His dad had said, "Stay off the cove ice. It's saltwater. It doesn't freeze the same as fresh." His dad said it every winter, but this past year was the first time Mason ignored him.

As he waded out into the water, his thoughts went back there, remembering how he and his friend Ben, who was only a little smarter than Mason, had wandered through the woods behind their houses. The boys were in seventh grade. They'd both been home alone for winter break.

For some reason their parents trusted them. Proof that even parents can be dumb.

The boys had been bored and drifting. They didn't talk about where they were going. They may have been willing to stay at Ben's house to play video games, but Ben's parents had taken his X-Box and locked it in a closet. He'd put a hockey puck through one of the windows in their basement and his mom was punishing him. Ben hadn't done it on purpose, but that didn't matter. "No electronics for a week," she'd said.

When the boys went outside, it was because they couldn't think of anything else to do. The backyards they'd grown up with failed to become more interesting as they got older. The boys made a weak attempt at playing, swinging at each other with sticks, but as soon as Ben got his knuckles thwacked the game was over.

It's a terrible thing, but at a certain age it's not as easy to pretend you're a soldier or a knight anymore. Your imagination gets turned down and you say things like, "It's so unfair," about your locked-away game system.

Mason answered Ben with a snowball before crossing the street. He went down a hill to the stream bed. The water was barely running there, bubbling over the rocks. They ignored the fact that their boots were getting wet as they followed it out to the cove.

They turned the corner around the stream's bank to see a frozen wasteland stretched out in front of them. The ice went all the way to the mooring fields, where boats docked in the summertime. It was white and perfect. "We should go back and get some hockey sticks, then we could play," Ben said.

Mason looked at his friend, wondering how he could even talk with this view in front of him. He was thinking of arctic explorers and alien worlds, but all Ben cared about was sports? It was the great void of their friendship. "You want to play with just the two of us?" Mason asked.

Ben shrugged. He loved hockey but he couldn't skate to save his life. "It could still be fun," he said.

Mason's father's warning echoed back in his head. He heard it, clear as could be, then he swiftly ignored the caution, feeling a thrill as he said, "Let's check it out." He jumped, coming down hard to test the ice. They were still close to the shore, so when it snapped and broke under him, his foot touched the ground. He stepped out a little farther and jumped again. This time the ice held.

Ben was behind him, moving more slowly. Perhaps it was because he was smarter than Mason, or maybe it was because he was tall and a little clumsy. That's why he wasn't good at skating. Either way, when Mason waved his arm and said, "Come on, man," Ben fell in line.

Their boots were slipping as they moved. "How far do you wanna go?" Ben asked. He had his arms out. He looked like an airplane coming in on a windy day. The idea of playing hockey was gone.

Mason didn't answer. Out on the ice it was incredibly quiet and peaceful. He didn't want to break the silence. And yes, that was the last thing he should've been worried about breaking. He was looking out at the mouth of the cove, at the horizon beyond him. It tempted him. The poor kid didn't know this was going to be the story of his life.

"Hey, I think I might be good with this," Ben called, still lagging behind.

"Oh, come on, just a little farther," Mason said over his shoulder.

Ben knew Mason wasn't going to back off. "Why don't we head over to the park?" he said. He figured it'd be a compromise and it would get them closer to shore.

Mason stared out for a moment more. It's strange how water can call to you. Some people are scared of it, others like Mason are enchanted, and a lot of people like Mason also end up drowning.

Mason turned and looked at Ben, who didn't look nearly as tranquil, then he looked at the tall trees that lined the edge of the state park. There was a small forest that ran all the way to the point.

"Yeah, okay," Mason said, taking pity on his friend. He'd been through those woods so many times, but he'd never come to them walking on water. They skidded and slid toward the trees, moving slowly. They were twenty yards out and smelling the pines when the ice softened. The boys didn't know that the ice near shore was the most dangerous. They didn't know how deep the water was either, but they'd soon find out.

Ben was the first one to feel the cracking. "Whoa, check it out," he said, stepping farther, still heading toward the woods. The crack became larger, splitting the ice into separate sheets.

Never once did they think, 'Let's be careful.' Instead, nearly at the same time, they both thought, 'Run!'

Ben was long and lean. His strides got him to the shore quickly. Mason was stout, solid and heavy, like a rock. That didn't help on the ice.

One long sheet lifted up as Mason fell. It happened so fast. Mason slid between the two pieces while his hands scrambled across the surface. He couldn't stop himself. Icy water splashed up into his face, stinging him. As the water covered his head, he took a deep breath, then he was under.

Mason could feel the edges of the ice slipping from his hands. His clothes were soaked and heavy, clinging to his body and weighing him down. Panic was all he was capable of as he sank deeper. Then, in a heartbeat, his thoughts slowed. His foot touched something. It was solid and strong. Everywhere else the cove was covered in muck. That's why no one swam there, but this thing was hard. He wondered what it could be as his lungs began to burn.

He looked up at the ice and saw the sun shining through the surface. It wasn't far. The cracks had spread. He looked for the largest to try and escape through. He pushed off from the solid thing with all his strength, shooting up above into the fresh air. If his foot had touched the muck, he wouldn't have escaped, only this firm thing made pushing off possible.

As he took a breath, he tried to grab the sheet of ice, but it was too slippery. His gloved hands were useless. He was kicking his legs, trying to tread water, breathing hard and fast. He pushed forward and got his belly on the ice, landing like a seal, but he couldn't stay that way. Every time he stopped moving, stopped kicking his legs, he'd slide back, going in again.

The shore looked so close, but there was no way through the shattered, slushy ice field. Those broken pieces trapped him and he'd soon be exhausted. "Help!" he called.

Ben was already halfway back into the water, trying to get to his friend. He'd come out as far as his waist, moving through the slurry and chunks. Any farther and he'd drown, too.

"I can't," Ben said, pushing the ice out of his way. He was doing the best he could, but he was almost more scared than Mason. He knew his mom would kill him if he let his best friend die and then his X-Box would be locked away forever.

"Get something," Mason called, still trying to pull himself up and feeling himself slip back every time he stopped.

Ben nodded his head and ran back to the shore. There were branches broken at the edge of the woods. He grabbed the longest and hurried back into the water. He reached out and Mason took hold. They both pulled at the same time. Mason and the sheet of ice moved through the broken chunks, slipping over the water until he felt his feet drag on the bottom. He tried to stand and nearly fell over again. His body was so cold.

Ben grabbed his arm and helped him to the water's edge, where he took out his phone. His parents had told him it was for emergencies only. This seemed to fit the bill.

"What are you doing?" Mason asked, seeing it.

"Calling for help," Ben answered while taking off on of his gloves to dial. The phone was wet but it still seemed to work.

Mason reached out and covered the keypad. Through chattering teeth he said, "No, don't. I'll be alright. Let's just get home, okay?" He didn't give Ben time to argue, but started walking instead, struggling not to stumble.

Ben watched him for a moment. He was convinced that they should call for help, but he also knew what his mom would say. "I'm getting rid of your X-Box all together. It's going in the trash," as if any of this had been the games system's fault. 'Mom logic,' Ben thought.

He put his phone away and hurried to catch up just as Mason started to run.

"Hey, why are we racing?" Ben called behind him. Mason was pumping his arms and legs, not to beat his friend home, but to try and stay warm. He was also concerned that if he moved too slowly the water in his clothing would freeze and he'd be stuck out in the woods like a statue.

"I'm cold," Mason called over his shoulder as they reached the road.

"Yeah, obviously," Ben said. They were farther from home than they thought, having walked so far across the ice. With every car that passed, they worried that some nosy, helpful person would stop and ask if they were alright. Luckily there were no good-hearted people around. After a while, their run became more of a jog and eventually a quick walk. They came to the woods behind their houses and cut through the trees.

Mason ran up onto the deck and pushed open the kitchen door. Before he was even through, he started taking off his clothes. Ben stayed outside, turning his back, embarrassed by the speed with which his friend got undressed. "Thanks for the help," Mason said over his shoulder, struggling to get his jeans off.

"Yeah, so, um, I'm going to go," Ben said, turning to walk away. "You going to be alright?" he called.

"I'll take a hot shower," Mason said, still trying to get his jeans off. They were clinging to him like hungry eels. He turned and looked at his friend with his pants halfway down his legs. "You're not going to say anything, are you?"

Ben shook his head, surprised he'd even asked. "Are you out of your mind, of course not? Even if you had died, I probably would've kept my mouth shut."

"Oh," Mason said, raising his eyebrow.

"I'm kidding."

Mason wasn't so sure. His squished down his jeans, then sloshed a trail of water across the tiles as he went over to a chair and sat down.

"I'll see you," Ben said, waving as he left. His pants legs were frozen stiff. He looked like he had no knee caps as he walked. Mason watched through the window to make sure his friend got home okay. Then he climbed in the shower and sat on the floor. He watched the water go down the drain. He should've been thinking about how close he'd come to dying, but whenever he remembered being under the ice his only thought was, 'What was that thing I touched?' He wanted it to be something special.

Months passed and he never talked to Ben about the thing under the water. Not even when Ben brought that day up, saying stuff like, "I really thought you were dead. That would've sucked."

Mason agreed with him. Being dead would've sucked. But he still didn't like talking about it. Ben, on the other hand, really enjoyed telling the story. He'd hold court, telling anyone who'd listen, especially at lunchtime. Mason let him have his glory. After all, he had saved his life so he deserved some credit. Eventually, after about a week, the story had been told and their middle school moved on to some other drama. It was forgotten by everyone but Mason, who was only waiting for the water to become a little warmer.

'And I should've waited even longer,' he thought, as he took one more step out into the cove. He pulled his mask down, took a breath and then flopped down into the salty water.

He swam out till his feet couldn't touch bottom, then he took a breath and pushed himself down. Finally, being like a rock came in handy. He reached out, touching the bottom, finding the muck. It was incredibly gross.

He came back up and looked at the trees, trying to remember. He thought back on what he'd seen that day. Which one had been in front of him? He pictured them covered in snow instead of leaves. When he thought he found the spot he dove down again.

He swam farther, feeling like he was plunging to the bottom of the ocean, even though it was only a few feet. He reached out, touching more muck, searching. Then he felt it, that solid thing that saved his life. It being there had given him something to kick off of. Without it, and with the weight of his clothes, there would've been no hope. The muck would have held him there.

He grabbed the thing and pulled himself lower. He held his breath till it burned as he searched along its length, feeling its edges. He understood what it was that saved him and he felt a thrill.

He swam up and went back to the beach. There was a long summer in front of him and he couldn't wait to tell Ben what they'd be doing. He had a mission.

The thing under the water was a sunken boat. Mason didn't know how he was going to do it, but he knew, whatever it took, he'd bring it back to the surface. He thought back to that day on the ice, before everything went bad. He had looked at the open mouth of the cove and felt it calling to him. He heard it again.

Gifted

by Jack Nolan

Tommy Hannigan smacked his fat hands together to keep them from numbing up and stomped his ragged sneakers against the frozen ground, but his feet were already dead meat. At last his brother Jimmy emerged from the muddy thicket of brush beneath the bridge that spanned the Merrimack River. Tommy told him, "Ya look a wreck, ya." From knees down, Jimmy's jeans and shoes were thick with icy muck and black smudges decorated his face, hands and hooded sweatshirt.

"Had to be done," Jimmy said, "and you wouldn't do it."

"I got more sense than to wade a swamp, dead of winter. Find anythin'?"

"I wasn't looking for *anything*, Tom. I was looking for one thing, and I apparently did not find it."

Since Jimmy was the smartest guy Tommy knew — smarter than all the brothers and sisters in the whole Hannigan tribe put together, way too smart to be a son of the drunk they all called "Our Alleged Father," and probably smarter than anyone who had ever attended Our Lady of Sorrows High School — whenever Jimmy cooked up one of his crazy plans, Tommy went along. "There are lots of bags and papers and any one of them might be it," Jimmy told him. "We need to retrace his steps, get inside his head, think like he thinks."

But searching out here on a viciously cold, windy day like this for one lousy, lost lottery ticket, wading under muddy bridges and digging through stinking garbage bags, this was pushing Tommy's limit.

The plan had been outlined in detail in Jimmy's neat handwriting before they set out. It began: "Thesis: The person who bought the lottery ticket at Dante's Liquor on June 5 also bought booze. No one has stepped forward to claim the 6.1 million dollars, so it was probably bought by some drunken idiot who doesn't remember buying it. First Corollary: Since O.A.F. fits that description and buys from Dante's and gets drunk on the way home, drinking out of the bag in the car or under some tree or bridge, and since Ma always checks pockets before washing pants, if O.A.F. asked for a ticket and the clerk dropped it in the bag, it could still be there, lying on the ground. Second Corollary: It could be someone else just like him."

Following this thesis statement was a list of twenty-four places to be checked discreetly, leaving nothing disturbed or out of place, around the house, garage and car. Then a drawn map of the area around Dante's, marked off in concentric circles with forty-two likely spots to check, and then a to-do list of how to manage the ticket, if found, to try to assure the money benefited all the Hannigan children. Priests, cops, and lawyers were eliminated in favor of Auntie Susan as the best choice of someone who would pose as the winner and be what Father Crowley called "a faithful steward." She was the closest thing to a trustworthy adult they knew of, she tried to do things for her nieces and nephews, and she hated her brother-in-law and wasn't afraid of him. The list was systematically checked off as the two of them carried out the mission, spotting for each other, working behind the backs of the loud, teeming mass of their family in the close quarters of the small house. Many of the items 1 through 24 proved tricky, and now they were working the concentric circles, which presented its own set of challenges, including this one, premised on some drunk tossing the bag out of a car window on the bridge near Dante's that would have landed in the wild brush under the bridge.

"What's next, Tommy?"

The appointed bookkeeper for Project Eureka pulled dog-eared pages out of his hip pocket and read, "Field off Pine Street...some day when it's warm. What's Eureka mean?"

"Means ' I found it,' something I picked up in Sister Phil's math class. And we can't wait until it's warmer or it may be beyond recovery. Here's the take: A nice day in June, those trees overlook the river and if our mystery subject wanted a pleasant spot to sit out of view of the road, that's one chance. It's on the way straight from Dante's to our house. I think we're about to get lucky, Tom, we're red-hot now because we have already eliminated so many other possibilities. We're on the short list now."

"I gotta get home, Jimmy. I gotta get warm, not red hot, and what if some old lady put that ticket through a washing machine back in June and we're out here for nut'in...."

"Don't talk that way. I told you, you're being defeatist. We're not quitting."

"Okay, look. Even if you're right about all of it — that it's layin' around somewhere — how the hell we gonna find it even so? It's prob'ly in the river."

That's what this heavy-set, wide-shouldered seventh-grader said, but the truth of his heart was that he took great pride in being trusted by his big brother, "The Brain" of Lowell, Massachusetts, who had chosen him over four older, more athletic brothers and two sisters to be his partner in what he called "a confidential quest." Jimmy seemed grown-up to him already, headed for great things, skipping second grade in school, getting special attention from teachers. Magical is how Jimmy seemed to him, if a little crazy sometimes.

They jogged down Pine Street to get warm, wrapping their bare hands inside their ragged, hand-me-down sweatshirts — a lanky, loose-jointed kid, author of dozens of pages of detailed plans for his future life, which would be lived far away from Lowell, beside his squat bowling-ball of a brother, dim-witted and loyal as a dog.

Likely Spot #33 was a treasure trove: paper and plastic bags, empty bottles, many from liquor stores. Jimmy organized a sweep pattern, cutting swaths one yard wide, up and back, "like mowing a lawn," he told Tommy. Wrappers, receipts, and scratch tickets were plentiful but only one of the machine-generated lottery slips was found, pulled out of a paper bag, stuck to the side of an empty bottle of cheap whiskey. Tommy handed it to his brother, who said quietly, "You found it. This is it." Then they exploded in a screaming dance, leaping and punching the air. "Eureka! Eureka!" answered by "We're rich! We're rich!" Finally, exhausted, they sat on the hard ground, handing their great prize carefully back and forth and repeating the numbers aloud to be sure they weren't dreaming it.

"What we gonna do now? We hide it?"

"We follow the plan, just like it's written out. We take this out to Auntie Susan and we do it now, today, and we put our trust in her."

"How we do that? Your bike's broke and the roads are an icy mess."

"We walk it. I looked it up. It's twelve miles on back roads. We get there tonight, maybe seven, eight o'clock if we start now. We lay everything out to her and beg her to help us. She phones Ma to say we're spending the night and if we can get an early bus and get to school tomorrow, maybe we don't get whipped too bad when we get home." Jimmy laughed. "All the times we been beat for nothing — this time it'll be completely worth it!"

"What ya got there?" brought them to their feet. Three kids, strangers, came toward them across the field, each as tall as Jimmy.

"We found some booze," Jimmy told him, holding up the empty pint. "Drank it."

"No, you didn't, you lyin' punk. We saw you found some money. So hand it over." He pointed at Jimmy's muddy jeans, to show he had watched him pocket the ticket there.

Jimmy denied having anything, but his voice was beginning to shake and the three were fanning out, ready to run them down. *If I run,* Jimmy thought, *they'll get Tommy.*

"Leave my brother alone." Tommy's voice rang strange in Jimmy's ears, full of calm authority, as though it were coming from someone else.

"Stay outta this, shorty, or I'll rip your head off your—" Before he finished, Tommy pounced into his legs with astonishing speed, locking his knees and dragging him down. His two friends struggled to pull Tommy off their leader, but he yanked his right arm free and drove a teeth-shattering roundhouse into one kid's face. The leader was back up now and rushed into the fight. Tommy buried a fist in his gut, bringing his head in reach for a short left-right combination, which sounded like someone splitting a watermelon with a cleaver. The leader crawled away from Tommy on his hands and knees, drooling blood into the grass; his other victim sat very still, holding his jaw in place with blood-soaked fingers. "You want yours too?" Tommy quietly asked the third.

Nothing more was said until the brothers climbed back onto the road from the open field. "Lotta help you were," came in that same calm, forceful voice Jimmy had trouble recognizing as his brother's.

"Jesus, Thomas!" Jimmy said. "Who taught you to fight like that!"

"You're a smart guy. I can punch," Tommy said, beaming. "We all got our gifts."

Hope Springs Eternal

by Hank Ellis

We were warned, but we didn't believe the rumors. How could it be that bad? I guess it didn't matter because we had no choice. Or maybe I should say, my son had no choice. I could have stayed home and avoided the entire matter. But he needed to finish something he had started quite some time ago. And I knew he could use the support. I had his back. If he went down, I was going with him.

As I think back about it, there should have been a sign over the entrance: Abandon hope, all ye who enter here.

The first hour was expected. We entered a long serpentine line that wound back and forth at least five times. A baby was crying and several young kids were fidgeting in line. I felt bad for the mothers dealing with the unfortunate experience on their own. I suspect newcomers to the situation were hopeful the line would move quickly. Some people would make eye contact and others wanted nothing more than solitude and conclusion. The wait was becoming burdensome.

Halfway through the second hour people were getting agitated. The line had moved, but not nearly as fast as anticipated. Waiting to move forward, we could hear conversations in the adjacent lines. People were complaining to one another. Some were calling on cell phones to tell others they were going to be longer than expected or they called simply to pass the time. My son and I talked and joked about anything and everything. We were not about to lose all hope.

It was probably near the end of the second hour that we finally reached the counter—the place where a person would solve our problem. The endless wait was finally over! It's good that hope springs eternal because we soon discovered this was only a checkpoint—a place to determine if we had all the necessary information for our business. We were given a number and told it would be called. The line behind us remained as long as ever and the one in front had now scattered throughout the room—every man, woman, and child on their own. People were spread out on the floors because all seats and windowsills were already taken. The wall became a premium for people who needed back support.

The third hour was not expected. Numbers came and went at a snail's pace. We started up a conversation with a man sitting next to us on the floor. He clearly didn't want to be there either, but he laughed with us. As I sat on the floor, I thought it ironic that a state with the word HOPE emblazoned on its flag continued such an onerous system—a system that affected so many people. Maybe those who adopted the motto back in 1664 were preparing us for the future.

My son and I still had that hope—albeit quite different from the founders. Our hope envisioned a fitting end to this interminable wait. Maybe not as grand and lofty as the hope that resided in the minds of our founders, we entered this place in the hope that lines would move quickly, that we would be treated fairly, and that our business would be concluded in a positive manner.

Unfortunately, fatigue has a way of sapping the hope from the best of us. We were both tired. Me, because my lower back was hurting and my son because he has a new family and works hard at what he does. I looked around the room knowing that everyone else, in some degree, was experiencing the same tiredness. Near the end of the fourth hour we were frustrated. It wasn't obvious that a good outcome was assured.

But then it finally happened—our number was called. Our faces withheld any sign of celebration because we had watched many faces before us. Some were jubilant and others were fit to be tied after they had finished their business. We couldn't imagine waiting more than four hours only to be told "I'm sorry." Not knowing what to expect, we approached the small cubicle with apprehension.

When the man behind the desk smiled, we knew—we knew that he understood what we had endured over the last four hours. His helpful and caring attitude made our wait bearable. I wondered if we were lucky. Perhaps things might not have gone as well with another person. We were thankful he wasn't irritable, tired, or angry and that we had enough energy to engage in a positive manner. It's amazing what a kind word, smile, or helping hand will do.

Leaving the building at the end of the day, I couldn't help but look back at the top of the doorway and think—I guess things can always be worse.

Promise Song

by Debbie Kaiman Tillinghast

Solitude cries into the night
Like the call of a distant loon,
Morning wakes, yawning its light,
And the daffodils still bloom.

Winter lingers without care,
Rain drops drum an angry tune.
North winds leave the branches bare,
But the daffodils still bloom.

Weeds of worry choke the view
Of more healing days to come,
Lilacs scent the softening air,
And the daffodils still bloom.

Empty places fill the pews,
Prayers are said in separate rooms,
Thoughtful hands reach out to share,
And the daffodils still bloom.

Sunshine soothes the troubled soul
When pain and sorrow loom,
Love is sent from far away,
And the daffodils still bloom.

The porch swing creaks a promise song,
Someone will sit beside me soon,
Fireflies blink the end of day,
And the daffodils always bloom.

Behind the Veil of Death

by R.N. Chevalier

It is 3:00 a.m. when I'm rushed into the ER with injuries sustained in a car accident. My body is broken - my legs, my chest, and my head. My internal organs are bruised and ripped. I lost two pints of blood at the scene before the ambulance arrived and I flatlined in the ambulance, twice, en route to the hospital.

As I'm being wheeled into the operating room, my torn flesh already shows a bluish hue as the cells within my body become more deprived of oxygen and start to die. I feel the heat escape as the cold fingers of death wrap tighter around my soul.

I look around as four masked strangers struggle to stop the bleeding and stabilize my vital signs, which are dropping quickly. I look up and focus on the two dish-shaped lights over the heads of the doctors. As my eyes slowly close, the bright light steadily changes to a darker shade, ending in utter blackness.

I am aware of voices. Commands called out. Questions asked. Answers given. I am only vaguely aware of the direness in all of the voices.

I hear the beeping of the monitor. I hear my heart beating electronically as the voices continue. I hear the tones slow down as seconds tick by. The slow beeping sounds become a steady tone.

At 3:45 a.m. the doctor on duty calls it, my death. My life officially ends as I hover above the bed that my now lifeless corpse rests upon. I reflect on the events that led to this moment.

I will myself to the floor and suddenly find myself standing beside the bed. I stare into my own lifeless eyes yet feel nothing as I now know that death is not the end. Accepting, within my own mind, that my life is over allows the vortex to the next existence present itself.

Light begins to emanate from everywhere, from everything. Within seconds the light envelops all that I see. Its brilliance is overwhelming, yet I feel coolness within my eyes and not the burning one would normally expect, but again, nothing is normal anymore.

The brilliance begins to subside and is replaced by a spectacle that I find ineffable yet vaguely, hauntingly familiar, if only I could remember. I slowly come to realize that I had been living in a cloud of ignorance that is unveiling itself, only too slowly for my impatient mind.

I realize the darkness around me is having a strange, profound effect on my mind. My thought processes begin to slow down as comfort overcomes me. I drift into a state of relaxation that I've never experienced before. Yet, I think I have.

I drift into a chamber that's larger than the universe itself. Evenly spaced on both sides of me are rows of huge, glowing, milky-white orbs. The rows go on as far as I can see, forward and back, left and right, and up and down.

Surrounding the orbs are hundreds of oval energy pulses, moving from orb to orb. As I look across the expanse, time slows down in my mind. Euphoria embraces me with a familiar warmth.

I have a sudden realization that there are more, many more, chambers like this one but I don't understand how I know this. Like before, by will alone, I find myself in another chamber identical to the first. I watch as the oval energy pulses float between the orbs. I see clusters of pulses in between the orbs.

I will myself to another chamber. The energy pulses seem more familiar but I still don't know why. That's not entirely correct, as I do know why they seem familiar, I just can't remember. Frustration sets in but the calmness of my surroundings overcomes the negativity.

I allow myself to travel along a corridor between the orbs. My curiosity overtakes me. I get close to the orb nearest me. Within the milky whiteness is a vision. I see people passing by. I see hands, more people, and everyday objects. All these things are passing by at an incredible speed.

As I watch, I realize that I'm watching a life, a human life, from birth to death. I travel to the next orb. This orb shows a different life, as do all of the orbs.

I see male and female lives. I see lives from tens of thousands of different species from across all of the universes. I see lives spanning all of the centuries before where I was and all of the centuries after. Now the understanding of this place becomes clear.

I approach a cluster of energy pulses that I now know are like me.

"How was your ride?" I understand one of the pulses say without words.

"It was very intense," I reply.

"What did you go as?" comes from another.

"Male," I answer. "A human male."

"That's what I was," the first one responds. "Well, kind of. I was a human female."

"What era were you in?" I ask.

"The turn of the twenty-first century," the first one replies. "I was a therapist."

"We met," I say, as the memories come rushing into my consciousness. "I got an illness in the third quarter of my ride. At the time we met I knew you but couldn't remember from where."

"Wow!" the first one answers. "That was you? I remember that. I remember the pandemic as well. Wasn't that whole time tumultuous?"

"It was," I tell him. "But I loved every minute of it. The only thing I didn't like was not remembering all of it, but it did make the ride so much better."

"Do you know what you're going as next?" a third asks.

"A Tankarian female," I answer. "I want to experience being a quadruped this time. What are you going as?"

"I'm going to earth this time," another answers. "I'm going to be the first woman to walk on their moon."

"Sounds like fun."

"Have a good time," they say as they drift away.

"Thanks, I will. Enjoy your rides. I'll see you all when we're done."

I drift toward the orb that I was watching before running into the group. I enter the glowing orb and my surroundings become milky white. The glowing brightness fades to black. I float in the dark silence for several seconds before I feel a pulling force. I feel constricted as I try to open my eyes but to no avail. The pulling force stops after a time and I open my eyes to see a masked person over me.

I am lifted and wrapped in a soft, warm blanket. I look up to see a woman staring back at me, making strange faces at me. I let out a cry to announce my arrival… my birth.

How Screen Time Created Intimacy

by Bary Fleet

When I learned that I was being given a week to create - and teach in - a virtual classroom, I began kicking and screaming like a spoiled child! I have been teaching as an adjunct professor for over thirty years and I am very comfortable doing things the old-fashioned way, teaching in a real classroom with desks and chairs, with a lectern and chalkboard. (Okay, I actually like the innovation of the whiteboard, because that allowed me to spice up my notes and illustrations with colored markers instead of the monotone white chalk.) But this virtual thing got to me!

I started collecting Social Security years ago, and my wife keeps asking me when I'm going to retire. My answer is always the same: "When it stops being fun, or when my student evaluations go south." I'd like to think that I will recognize when I stop being effective as a teacher, but it really is the students' evaluations that matter.

Well, having to transition to teaching in a virtual classroom was not fun!

"I'm ready to quit," I told my wife, and I meant it.

Sure, there were some bumps in the road, some hiccups along the way, but I learned enough about the new technology to make it work.

The more I used Zoom, the more I began to see some advantages. Don't get me wrong: I would much rather be teaching the old-fashioned way instead of virtually, but there were some pleasant surprises.

I did set up the virtual classroom so that we would meet synchronously, which meant that all the students were required to be present in real time. I was awed when I realized that, while many of my students live in the northeast, I had one student in Hawaii and another student in

Istanbul, and we were all in class at the same time! Kudos to their commitment to their education.

I also realized that students were more likely to participate in class discussions in the Zoom Room than they would have been in the traditional classroom. I attributed that to the fact that every student was looking at every other student's face; it was as if we had formed a big conversation circle. When I asked for their observations, they reported that they felt emotionally safer speaking from their own homes than they did in a formal classroom. (Note to self: How do I, as a professor, create a greater sense of emotional safety in the traditional classroom?)

One of the ironies of the virtual classroom was that it created more intimacy. Part of this is attributable to the fact that in the traditional classroom, from the time students arrive until I call the class to order, they are all checking their phones. In the Zoom Room, when they log in, they are looking at the computer screen and each other's faces. We were able to have informal conversations with each other. I could ask how their day was going, what challenges they were facing, how they were coping with the 'shelter in place' restrictions, etc.

The other aspect of the sense of intimacy was the fact that I could literally see into their homes, as they were able to see my home office. Some were ensconced in the coziness of their bedrooms, others on the couch in their living rooms, while yet others were at the kitchen table. (I did request that none of them publicize the fact that they had met with their professor in their bedrooms!)

Another happy incident was when I was teaching my students about the importance of their parents having a written will, Proxy for Health Care, Durable Power of Attorney, and Advance Directive. One of my students immediately yelled to her mother in the next room, asking if she had those. The mother spontaneously came in and joined the Zoom Room, and I was able to have a conversation with a member of my students' parents' generation about her experience with the death of her mother (my student's grandmother). It proved to be enriching and insightful for the entire class, something that would never have occurred had we been in a traditional setting.

In the end, I believe we all knew each other at a much deeper level than we ever would have - all because of screen time!

The moral of the story: Before you complain too much about having to change, try it - you might like it!

About the Authors

David Boiani is an American author living in Coventry, Rhode Island. He writes psychological thrillers and has five books published, with another, *Azreal's Ledge*, due to be released by the end of the year.

His works include his first book, *A Thin Line*, and its sequel *The Redemption*, short story collection *Dark and Darker Musings*, and his latest release, *Immortal*. His short story "The Game of Kings" was included in the 2019 ARIA anthology.

Visit his website at www.authordavidboiani.com. Sign up for his newsletter here: https://landing.mailerlite.com/webforms/landing/r8i8i7, where you will receive updates, news, and special content and offers.

Judith Boss has had several short stories published, including "A Slice of Life" in *Bewildering Stories Magazine*, "Francine" in *Thinking: Philosophy for Children*, and "The Cornfield," which appeared in *Blood Moon: Best New England Crime Stories.*

In addition to writing short stories, she has two novels - *Deception Island* and *Fall From Grace,* both of which were published by Wild Rose Press. She has also written four college textbooks for McGraw-Hill, two of which are among the top sellers in their fields.

After leaving the U.S. Air Force, **R.N. Chevalier** had a series of jobs, including musician, private investigator, and professional mover. He married Donna Fluette in 1993 and their daughter, Jasmine (or Jay as she prefers) was born in 2000 in St. Petersburg, Florida.

He was diagnosed with ALS in 2012 and officially retired in 2014. His first novel, *Are We the Klingons*, was published in 2015. He wrote *Advances of the Ancients* and *Full Circle,* which were published in 2016 and 2017, respectfully.

In 2018, he and his wife Donna published *Rhode Island Civil War Monuments - A Pictorial Guide*. A book about the Massachusetts Civil War monuments has been delayed due to the pandemic but is scheduled for a 2021 release. In 2019, he wrote his first children's sci-fi book, *Jay and Rowan - In Time*, which was illustrated by his daughter Jay.

Other projects include a collection of short stories, Civil War monuments of Connecticut and a spin-off from *Are We the Klingons*. As for now, his ALS is progressing at a very slow rate and he is hopeful that a cure is forthcoming.

Jess M. Collette has always loved to write. Whether for an assignment, something special for a family member or just for fun, she's filled many pages. In honor of her son, Joshua, she published the children's book on love and loss, *Your Special Star*. Shortly after, she published her debut novel, *Naming the Bits Between*, an uplifting fictional adventure book. In addition to writing, she also makes unique creations with graphic design. Jess lives in Rhode Island with her husband and their adorable rescue dog from Texas. Visit www.jessicamcollette.com to view her current writing, poetry, and designs.

Belle A. DeCosta is the creator and director of Tap N Time, a seated tap and rhythm class designed for the elderly. When not traveling to nursing homes to share her program, she enjoys being in nature, dining with friends, and writing.

Belle shares a home in East Providence, Rhode Island, with her beloved hound, J.D., and an aquarium full of assorted fish.

Kevin Duarte first had a poem published in the Roger Williams University anthology when he was a senior. In his late twenties, a local company produced a comic book called "P.R.I.M.E.," which he wrote with a friend. The comic was produced and sold quite well in the local area, garnering local TV coverage at one of the book signings in a local comic book store.

He is currently working on two novels, *Manifest Destiny*, which he hopes to complete by the end of the year, and *Flashpoint*, a new thriller. Kevin enjoys writing speculative fiction as well as fantasy. He is inspired by the human collective, both good and bad, and loves to create characters as much as he loves to create and modify the world around them.

Hank Ellis is a retired environmental scientist with degrees in natural resources and wildlife management. He's the author of *The Promise: A Perilous Journey* and *The Promise: Discovering Their Gifts* - the first two books in an environmental adventure series written for kids eight to one hundred and eight. He has written two other short stories that are featured in the 2018 and 2019 ARIA Anthology publications and is currently working on a third book in *The Promise* series.

Hank grew up in the wilds of Scituate, Rhode Island, where he gained respect for all living things (except maybe mosquitoes). From grade school though high school and even into his first year at the University of Rhode Island, he didn't think much about writing. Not until he joined the US Coast Guard and spent 10 months in Vietnam, where he kept a journal and sent letters home, did he have a desire to write well. It was when he returned to URI that his writing skill began to improve. The events in this short story are true. He'll let the reader be the judge of where they occurred.

Growing up as a middle child helped **Jill Fague** develop her independence. She now enjoys her career as an English teacher and favors some of the more spirited students in her classroom. Married for twenty years, Jill lives with her husband and two teenage children. The most recent addition to her family is an adopted grey tiger kitten, born with plenty of spunk.

With the publication of her memoir, *This Unfamiliar Road*, Jill shares her journey from breast cancer to battle scars and beyond. Proceeds from the sale of her book have been donated to the American Cancer Society.

In addition to being a pastor, **Bary Fleet** has spent more than 30 years teaching leadership and psychology at Emory University, Bryant University, and Johnson and Wales University. He is on the faculty of the Holmes Institute for Consciousness Studies and has been the program director for a non-profit counseling center. He is founder and director of the Institute for Inner Magnificence and is the author of the bestselling book *Move into Your Magnificence: 101 Invitations to a Life of Passion and Joy*. He currently has his own private consulting and coaching practice for individuals and corporations. He is a TEDx speaker and a Canfield Certified Success Coach.

Find out more at www.DrBaryFleet.com

Michael Geisser has been published in several journals, including *Monkeybicycle*, the *Journal of Microliterature*, the *Grub Street Daily*, *Flash Fiction Magazine*, *Sliver of Stone*, and *Intima: A Journal of*

Narrative Medicine. The author also contributed a chapter to the book, *Befriending Death*, by Vocino and Killilea.

He lives in Warren, Rhode Island, with his wife and their two dogs.

Douglas S. Levine is a physician scientist who resides in Seekonk, Massachusetts with his wife; they met in 1979 when they both worked at Rhode Island Hospital. His current day job is as a consultant in the life sciences sector, and his professional writing experience includes technical publications in peer-reviewed medical journals and book chapters dating back to 1976. The platform for Doug's belated efforts in fiction-writing is his previous forty-plus years working in health care: doing clinical research, developing new diagnostic and treatment interventions, providing medical care, and acquiring insights into patients' illness experiences. He recently completed his first novel and is at work on a second one, writing under the pseudonym, **Abraham Simon**. Doug is a first-year member of the Association of Rhode Island Authors and is grateful for the opportunity to write and submit his first short story, "Two Oaks," for the 2020 ARIA Anthology.

Richard Maule was born in Miami, Florida. After a 40+ year career in Christian ministry, counseling, and public speaking, he moved to Connecticut to write historical novels. His first book, *Moonlight Helmsman*, received critical praise and 8 national awards for historical fiction. His new book, *The Witch's Advocate,* has already received 4 national honors, including the 2020 Beverly Hills Book Award. Richard is enjoying his new life as an author. He especially likes doing historical research, meeting interesting people, and raising money for good causes. His two novels have generated over $60,000 in profits, all of which have been donated to various charities in New England.

Joann Mead has lived in four countries ranging from A to Z: America, England, Russia, and Zimbabwe. She is a writer, educator, researcher, and futurist. Her written works include bio-thriller and crime novels, short stories, screenplays, magazine articles, and publications in medical journals on disasters and weapons of mass destruction. Her writing is inspired by the places she's lived and traveled and life's adventures along the way.

Her mysteries and thrillers are connected by the "underlying crimes" of genetic design. *Underlying Crimes*, her first novel, is set in a tiny New

England state known for its culture of corruption. *Tiger Tiger* is an international bioterror thriller where a femme fatale scientist creates a deadly pandemic Tiger Flu virus and plots to target America. *Designer Baby*, set in the near future in Scandinavia and Rhode Island, speculates on the real and imagined possibilities of customized, gene-edited super-human babies and the creation of ethnic targeted weapons.

"Married in Moscow" is a short story from my soon-to-be-published collection. My short stories are a mash-up of memory, fiction, and non-fictional stories. When in doubt, I make it up. I like to inject humor and irony in what I conjure up. My scenarios may blur the lines between fact and fiction, but I believe that what is real can be imagined. And what is imagined can be real.

Jack Nolan is the author of two zany novels that capture the incandescent years 1967-68 with humor: *Vietnam Remix* and *There Comes a Time*. He lives with his wife, Patricia, in Providence.

Pete A. O'Donnell is the creator of Illadvisedstories.com, a story podcast with free and funny tales for kids. His first book, *The Curse of Purgatory Cove*, a pirate story set in Rhode Island, was released last year and received the Royal Dragonfly award for best new author. He's a firefighter/EMT in East Greenwich, Rhode Island, and holds a degree in journalism and creative writing from Queens University in Charlotte, North Carolina.

Steven R. Porter is the author of two novels: the critically acclaimed Southie crime-thriller *Confessions of the Meek & the Valiant*, and the award-winning historical novel *Manisses* inspired by the rich history of Block Island. He is also the co-author of *Scared to Death... Do It Anyway* a guide for individuals who suffer from anxiety and panic attacks.

Steven speaks frequently at schools and libraries about his books, trends in independent publishing, and on special topics in writing and book marketing. He served as Director of Advertising and Public Relations for the 176 store Lauriat's bookstore chain through the 90's, and today, he and his wife Dawn own Stillwater Books and the independent press, Stillwater River Publications, in Pawtucket, RI. He is founder and president of the Association of Rhode Island Authors (ARIA).

Theresa Schimmel is the author of four published children's books: *Sunny, The Circus Song, The Carousel Adventure,* and *David's War/David's Peace*. Her short stories and poems have been featured and won awards in literary magazines and newspapers. *Braided Secrets* is her debut adult/young adult novel.

After 26 years of classroom teaching experience, she worked as an early childhood educational consultant at the state and national level. Now, most of her free time is spent writing. Married with two adult sons and two grandchildren, she resides in Rhode Island with her husband, Steve. Her books can be purchased through www.tamstales.net or through www.amazon.com.

Alexander Smith has published fiction in "Flash Fiction Magazine," "Into the Void," "Short Edition," "Creative Writing Outloud," and in his book, *The Perfect Man and Other Stories of the Supernatural*. His work has won an honorable mention from the "Writers of the Future" contest. He works as a copywriter for a Fortune 10 company and lives in Providence, Rhode Island.

J. Michael Squatrito, Jr. is a resident of Tiverton, Rhode Island, and the vice-president of the Association of Rhode Island Authors. He has written four books in his *Overlords* fantasy book series and is the founder of SelfPublishingInsight.com, which he created to help those achieve their dream of becoming a published author. His sincere hope is to inspire everyone he meets to be creative and follow their dreams. Stay up to date with his events, new releases, and fan extras at www.TheOverlords.com.

www.facebook.com/TheOverlordsBookSeries
Twitter: @Overlords
Instagram: @mikesquatrito

Emily Tallman has wanted to be a storyteller since hearing her first bedtime fairytale. She asked for a word processor for Christmas at age four and has kept her promise to Santa by writing every day since.

Her first set of books has been set in motion with the *Monsters Within* series. Emily hopes to make mental illness a more readily accessible topic. Enjoy this behind the scenes look from Rose, a character in the upcoming *Monsters Within* novel entitled *Hair of the Dog*, coming Fall 2021.

Debbie Kaiman Tillinghast is the author of *The Ferry Home,* a memoir about her childhood on Prudence Island, a tiny island off the coast of Rhode Island. Debbie began writing when she embarked on a quest to reconnect with her island roots, starting with a cookbook for her family. A retired teacher and Nutrition Educator, Debbie now enjoys volunteering as well as writing, gardening, biking, and spending time with her grandchildren.

Barbara Ann Whitman is a seasoned social worker with experience as a child abuse and neglect investigator. She has worked professionally with hundreds of foster children, from newborn through young adult. Additionally, she has been a Sunday School teacher, a Youth group Leader, a parenting instructor, a Big Sister and a Girl Scout Leader. She founded a Meetup Group for active seniors in 2015, is a member of the Old Fiddlers Club of Rhode Island, where she also serves on the executive board. She sings in her church choir and belongs to a Celtic music group, and helps facilitate a writers' group at the local library.

Barbara Ann's writing falls across many genres. Her young adult novel *Have Mercy* is about a young woman's journey from the foster care system to adulthood. Her essays and poetry have been published in each of the previous ARIA Anthologies: "A Changing Sea" (2016), "Galilee" (2017), "A Crown of Diamonds" (2018), and "My Secret" (2019).

Follow her blog at www.rhodiebean.com.

ORDER FORM

Please use the following to order additional copies of

Past, Present & Future (2019), *Selections* (2018), *Under the 13th Star* (2017), and/or *Shoreline* (2016)
Selected Short Fiction, Nonfiction, Poetry and Prose from The Association of Rhode Island Authors

_____ (QTY) **Hope** X $10.00 Total $_______________

_____ (QTY) **Past, Present, and Future** X $10.00 Total $_______________

_____ (QTY) **Selections** X $15.00 Total $_______________

_____ (QTY) **Under the 13th Star** X $10.00 Total $_______________

_____ (QTY) **Shoreline** X $10.00 Total $_______________

**Shipping & Handling $_______________

GRAND TOTAL $_______________

**Shipping & Handling: Please add $3.00 for the first copy, and $1.50 for each additional copy.

Payment Method:

___ Personal Check Enclosed (Payable to ARIA)

___ Charge my Credit Card

Name:_______________ BILLING ZIP CODE:_______________

Visa____MC______Amex_____ Discover____

Card Number:_______________ EXP:______/_____CSC__________

Signature:_______________

<u>Ship To:</u>

Name _______________

Street _______________

City _______________State:_______________Zip:_______________

Phone _______________Email:_______________

___Check to add to ARIA's email list.

<u>MAIL YOUR COMPLETED FORM TO:</u>

The Association of Rhode Island Authors (ARIA)
c/o Stillwater River Publications
63 Sawmill Road
Chepachet, RI 02814
info@stillwaterpress.com
www.StillwaterPress.com
www.RIAuthors.org

Made in the USA
Middletown, DE
22 September 2021